I’m a Teller of Stories, Vol. 2

I’m a Teller of Stories

Volume II

Jim W. Powell

I'm a Teller of Stories, Vol. 2

ISBN: 978-1-951940-12-6 (Paperback)

Any references to historical events, real people, or real places are used fictitiously. Names, characters, and places are products of the author's imagination.

Interior images purchased from Vectorstock.com

Book design by Amanda Berkeley ~ Clarity Publishing Services, LLC.

Printed by Amazon KDP., in the United States of America.

First printing edition 2020.

Clarity Publishing Services, LLC
3199 Dellwood Ave. NW
Canton, OH 44708
Clarityservices.net

I'm a Teller of Stories
Volume II

by

Jim W. Powell

Contents

Preface and Acknowledgements 1

Introduction: My Hometown 3

A Haunted Bathroom 6

The Moving Man 15

Press the Button 23

Mrs. Palmer's Chickens 35

The Glory Days 47

Ghosts 55

Matthew and Julianne Collins 70

The Interloper 86

Gerald Moves On 94

Mr. Murphy's Garden 103

Jack Calloway 113

Miserable Charles 130

Mrs. Lewis 141

Day After Day 154

Allison Cried (A Vignette) 160

Preface And Acknowledgements

If you have read my first book, I thank you for honoring me with your purchase. Hopefully, you found my stories enjoyable and you should know that your support has inspired me to continue my writing endeavors.

I would like to use the remainder of this space to offer you a glimpse of what can be expected in the following pages. In this second book, I will be telling you just a little bit (I promise it will be quick and I won't bore you) about my hometown and then we will find ourselves imagining such things as:

A haunted guest bathroom, a trio of ghosts, an aunt and some mosquitos, a bizarre raccoon, some very badly-behaved chickens, a miserable retiree who seems to have lost his way, an old man missing his deceased companion dog, a well-meaning but somewhat over-zealous sales person, and other amusing and perhaps informative items of interest. I think you will enjoy the vignette as well.

As usual, the sun is casting a soft shade on my porch, the lemonade is on the table, my old dog is resting peacefully on his favorite rug, and now it's time to get this show on the road. I'm a teller of stories. Some might be true; some might be pure imagination—you decide.

My highly regarded editor and publisher, Amanda Lattavo Berkeley has done yet another outstanding job of bringing this book from a concept inside of my head to a finished creation on paper. And, as always, I am grateful for having been blessed with Sherri, my awesome and exceptional wife, who understands all of this. A large job, indeed! A VERY large job.

Read on, my friends.

My Hometown

I want to tell you briefly, *very briefly*, about my hometown – North Canton, Ohio. I was born here, but not literally born "here." My parents lived here on Bachtel Street when I came into the world, but my actual birth occurred in a hospital, south of this city. My parents were native to this city. In addition to my parents, grandparents and great-grandparents, there were aunts and uncles, cousins, extended family and many good friends and co-workers native to this city as well. I made my living in this city for 38 years. My daughter and I visited Dogwood Park countless times when we she was a child, and we skipped stones in a pond that is now the baseball field where the ferocious, imitation dogs struggle against the geese in an ongoing annual conflict with no foreseeable end.

This is a city where neighbors always say "Hello" and wave at you. This is a city where, if you are watering your front lawn, fetching your newspaper from the end of your driveway, or taking a walk, a police person will always wave at you when passing by. And if you engage a cop in conversation, he or she will always have time to chat with you. If you are injured or have become ill, the EMT people will be there to give assistance, not only because giving assistance to people in distress is their job, but because they truly live to serve. Likewise, the North Canton fire department is excellent. I know this because I have had job-related interaction with the NCFD personnel many times prior to my retirement in 2004, and I know that these fire and EMS folks are all stand-up people. They all make me proud to have been associated in some small way with them.

In this city, the proprietor of a nearby convenience store calls me "My Brother" and wants to know how I'm doing when I go there to purchase a lottery ticket or fill my tank. I know he really wants to know how we're doing, it's not just a casual phrase he throws out when he hears the bell ring above the door.

This is a city where you will see American flags on the old-fashion Main Street light poles every Fourth of July week. Not just a flag here and there, but flags lining the street all the way through the downtown area. I'm not ashamed to tell you that I get a lump in my throat and a feeling of pride in my city and in my country when I see this impressive display of patriotism every year. Most of the flags go away after the summer and are eventually replaced by holiday decorations – beautiful in their own right as well. The flags always return, though, every year, like the swallows returning to San Juan Capistrano, or the Monarch butterfly migrations.

There are ten parks here, which I think is remarkable considering that there are only around 18,000 residents in the city. We have two large community parks, along with eight smaller neighborhood parks. Our home is located two blocks from Dogwood Park and three blocks from the Fire/EMS station. Our city council person lives nearby in our neighborhood as well. According to a recent national ranking, North Canton is one of the best small-town cities to live in America. I agree.

I love this small blue-collar city of my heritage, home of hard-working people and home of the former Hoover Company, now gone forever, but always alive in my memories. I don't like to talk about the North Canton cemetery, as nice as it is; it's a great cemetery as far as cemeteries go, but we all know it's there – waiting. I wouldn't want to be anywhere else after . . . well . . . you know.

A Haunted Bathroom

Something unknown has been walking in and out of my guest bathroom. It has been doing this for around six weeks now and it's beginning to concern me – really! I know this sounds ridiculous to you but bear with me on this and I will explain everything. Before I start with the details of the unknown entity that is entering and withdrawing from my guest bathroom, it is necessary for you to have at least a rudimentary idea of where this bathroom is located in relation to my living area, which is where I always happen to be when I detect this bothersome commotion.

The living area is a rectangular space at the front of our house. If you were to sit in my favorite chair you would look straight ahead and you would see the TV atop a cabinet that sits against the wall, about ten feet from the chair. While you are looking at the TV, if you were to shift your eyes slightly to the right you would see a short hallway which stops at my office entrance. While you are looking at the hallway, you will see the guest bathroom door midway, on the right side. This door is where I see the arrivals and departures of the unknown visitor as it goes about its mysterious performances.

The thing – let's call this thing The Image – might be a ghost of some variation; but most likely not, although you never know. It doesn't stay in the bathroom very long. I would estimate the average visit is mere seconds at most. I hesitate to say that word "ghost" because I'm afraid this whole thing truly might be a classic case of bathroom haunting – the absolute worst kind of haunting. But, as a responsible teller of stories, I'm obligated to use the word ghost both aloud and on paper, so there can be no doubt of exactly what I am going to be discussing here.

I've never actually seen the face of The Image because its head and entire face are covered by what appears to be a hood. In fact, its entire body appears to be covered by a long, flowing robe, like what the grim reaper might wear on New Year's Eve, complete with a rope tied at the waist. The Image is also very tall. The top of its hood barely fits under the bathroom door frame. The Image is best described as semi-transparent, wispy and a light shade of beige, the color of heavy cream. Now, please don't misunderstand me. I'm certainly not suggesting that the image is, you know . . . using the bathroom. It seems to come out of the opposite wall, slithers across the hallway and through the bathroom doorway, then one or two seconds later, it slithers out and turns toward my office, gliding onward until it's out of sight. I'm quite sure The Image doesn't hang around in my office, though, and that's perfectly fine with me because I have work to do in there and I can't be distracted. I also don't feel comfortable imagining that something might be looking over my shoulder as I am working.

I've never seen The Image anywhere other than the bathroom and the hallway. I've been thinking that it seems to be looking for something. It appears that it enters the bathroom, perhaps looking around for whatever it is that it's trying to find, and then, after one or two seconds, it exits and goes away. Another possibility is that The Image might be routinely checking to see if the bathroom is being cleaned regularly; I can assure you; it is.

I see The Image only in the evenings while Sherri and I are watching TV. After my initial sighting, I casually mentioned the sighting of The Image to Sherri and she casually replied, "Oh, that's nice." Given her disregard of the sighting, I didn't follow through with giving her the full story, and she didn't inquire further. The next time it happened, I informed my wife that The Image had been in our guest bathroom again and she said, "Well, that's what guest bathrooms are for, Honey." She is not concerned, so I don't mention it anymore.

Since the first sighting, I'm guessing that there have been at least ten additional Image sightings to-date. What's the point to all this slithering and gliding in and out of bathrooms? If The Image is, in fact, searching for something, wouldn't we expect that The Image eventually would accept the fact that whatever it is looking for just isn't there? Just let it go. For all we know, whatever it is that The Image is looking for might be found next door, on Orchard Avenue, in the neighbor's guest bathroom, or just about anywhere else in North Canton for that matter, or possibly anywhere in the world, really. Perhaps The Image has been using incorrect map coordinates, or possibly struggling with a faulty ghostly compass.

Since sitting down here in my office to begin this story, I have already looked to my left towards the guest bathroom 14 times in the last 20 minutes and I can truthfully report to you that I've not seen anything suspicious from this particular vantage point. I know The Image is around here someplace, but for some reason it refuses to show itself to me when I'm closer to the bathroom than when I'm sitting in front of the TV. Maybe I should flip on the bathroom light switch and leave it on when I'm working in here.

I'm back at my desk. The bathroom light is on. This is ridiculous, I know, but it's going to get better as we read on.

It happened again last night, in the middle of watching NCIS! As usual, it drifted across the hallway and slithered into and out of the guest bathroom. Then, as usual, it turned toward my office and proceeded in the hall, until it was beyond my field of vision. This time I couldn't hold in my voice any longer, so I told Sherri about the ghostly vision and she replied, "Oh my." I said, "Really? That's all you're going to say?" She said, "Oh! You're serious? I thought you were talking about the car lights."

"What car lights?" I said, "What are you talking about?" "The neighbors," she said. "It's the neighbor's car turning into their driveway. You've never seen that?" I said, "Yes, of course I've seen that but I'm talking about something completely unrelated to the neighbor's headlights."

She further explained, "When they turn into their driveway, the headlights shine through our Venetian blind slats and then onto the wall in the hallway. But, you're joking, right?" I said, "Yes, Honey. Of course, I'm kidding you. I was just having some fun." She said, "You're funny."

I know my limitations, so . . .

Even though my wife's evaluation of these strange occurrences has been given for the record, I am not going to accept her explanation. I can't. It's just not good enough to prove anything one way or the other. As far as I'm concerned, her opinion on this matter just doesn't hold water. I have, in fact, seen the neighbor's occasional driveway "light show" many times. I'm convinced that these driveway lights are not in any way related to the guest bathroom mystery and they're not even remotely similar to the hallway/bathroom image. Not even close. Not even in the same ballpark.

There is no way to connect her lights to my image because I have seen The Image in the hallway several times when there were no neighbors pulling into or out of their driveway. And, my Image is soft and wispy and semi-transparent, while her lights are bright and glaring and annoying – reflecting on the wall behind the TV and on parts of the kitchen wall as well. In other words, not semi-transparent, and not anywhere near the bathroom area. My translucent image sightings began only about six weeks ago. I've been watching the driveway lights since we've lived here.

After explaining the above details to Sherri, she conceded that perhaps (perhaps) there is something other than car headlights in play here. "You have a good point." she said, "We have been here for a long time, and your sightings began only six weeks ago." Then she asked me to explain The Image again in more detail. I explained The Image details in the same fashion as I have just explained it to you, then she said, "Explain semi-transparency. Give me a graphic example of what you mean." I said, "My Image is constantly in motion, slowly pulsating. It fades from almost solid to mostly transparent as opposed to your solid and bright headlights that are shining on the wall." She asked if there are any specific facial features. "No. There are none because the hood covers the face." I say.

She asked, "Please explain what you mean by pulsating." I told her that The Image seems like it's trying to fall apart – as though the pieces were all glued together, as in a large collage, and then they collapse and immediately reassemble to the original form when I blink my eyes.

She probed further, "Oh! You mean like when you told me you thought you might be seeing possible micro-debris from your LASIC lens implants? The doctor told you that there might be surgical debris trapped between the cornea and the lens? And that you can have it easily removed? And that this is a common problem and that it's nothing to worry about? And that you have not yet made the appointment?"

To these outrageous accusations I replied, "Yea! But this isn't surgical debris! I'm sure of that."

Sherri said, "Do you remember that time when you were sitting at the kitchen table, beside the window, during that February windstorm? Wind gusts up to 70 mph? And you told me that you just saw something very large and very dark and menacing fly past the window in the direction of North Main Street? And you talked about it for days – actually for weeks?"

"Yes" I said, "I remember the incident clearly."

She said, "So, you might also remember that a few days later you proclaimed that someone had stolen the grill cover? And you said, 'What kind of person would steal a guy's grill cover, anyway?'

"Yea, I remember that" I said.

And then I realized that she had, once again, trapped me in the corner – like a skilled fighter would cleverly maneuver his opponent into the corner ropes while punching him in the kidneys several times before the referee is able to get them separated.

Eye surgery debris, airborne grill covers (I'm still not convinced that it wasn't stolen), dissolving images, neighbor headlights, whatever happened to childhood awe and admiration for mystery? When I was a kid, a turtle crawling across the driveway was an army tank attacking the little enemies that lived in the grass. A picnic table in the back yard was the cockpit of a TWA Super Constellation midway between here, and Phoenix, at 20,000 feet, and I am at the controls. The upper branches in the big maple tree in my childhood backyard were the Empire State Building, and I am crawling to the top to do battle and save the world from Godzilla.

Why can't surgical debris simply be a ghostly apparition – everyone loves a good ghost story, right? And, why can't a flying grill cover be an enormous, angry monster chasing a pterodactyl flying dinosaur?

Why didn't I tie the grill cover more securely last Fall when I dragged it to the back of our lot for the winter? Why didn't I call the Ophthalmologist to schedule the simple procedure – less than one hour, Bada-Bing, and out the door?

One last thought, and I don't want to start a whole new story here, but – what if, when I go the Ophthalmologist for a diagnosis, it is discovered there is no micro-debris in my eye, and everything is normal? Then what?

I'm just saying, "Where do we go from there?"

Just a thought.

The Moving Man

Robert Peterson lives four houses up the street from me in a lovely home on an acre of well-kept grass with three pear trees at the back of his lot. Behind his house there is a rectangular building which Robert uses as a parking shelter for his moving truck. He also has a dedicated space within that building for his workshop because, Robert does all his own vehicle maintenance; he parks his riding mower and other tools and equipment there as well. He parks his Jeep Wrangler in a smaller garage which is attached to the opposite side of house.

Robert retired several years ago after working for 23 years as a professional mover at a moving company in the Canal Fulton, Ohio area, a few miles west of here. I have no idea what he did for a living prior to becoming a mover, but a guy at the Main Street Grille once told me that Mr. Peterson had retired from the Navy prior to joining the moving industry and ultimately starting his own moving company. That sounds realistic to me. If we add the two jobs together, we have a work history of 43 years, give or take, and I know that Robert is now 68 years of age so, yes, that's about right.

Mr. Peterson seems like a nice enough guy. I don't see much of him what with his business traveling and because he keeps to himself when he's not working. Nothing wrong with that; the man likes his privacy – I get it. I don't know if there is a Mrs. Peterson. I haven't seen any indications of there being a Mrs. Peterson but, certainly, that doesn't mean that there isn't one. I have considered the possibility that perhaps Mrs. Peterson, if there is such a person, travels with her husband when he is moving stuff. That would explain everything, but who cares what they do? It's their truck and their business and their time. I only mention these details because I suspect that some of you might be asking the same question and it's my job to keep you accurately informed. Rest assured, if I know something, you will know it as well. This is what I do. I bring the facts to you and you may do with these facts as you wish.

So, here is something that you might find intriguing. Last week I was talking to the guy who lives across the street from me, and he asked me if I was finding that my stuff was being tampered with. He told me that something unusual has been going on at his house and that some of the other neighbors are finding evidence of unusual activity as well. I must admit that his question bothered me because my wife and I had been experiencing some very bizarre activity on our property. I hadn't given much thought to this strange activity because, for one thing, nothing has been stolen. Also, when I see evidence of unusual activity, I simply write it off as a result of me being careless and/or forgetful. But knowing that neighbors are experiencing the same activity is not good news. This is very disturbing news.

Our unusual activity started about a six months ago, which is what our neighbors had noticed as well. My wife has told me that she has found items of furniture moved. On one particular occasion, a heavy recliner chair was relocated to the opposite side of our master bedroom. In other cases, furniture items had been moved only a foot or two from their original location. I asked her why she had never mentioned this activity and she informed me that she simply thought it was me moving the items when I used the vacuum cleaner. She explained that this sort of thing has been occurring for at least six months but, knowing me as she does, she had been thinking of it as nothing out of the ordinary. Further, I noticed that our patio furniture had been moved around – on three separate occasions. I just assumed that Sherri had rearranged the stuff and never gave it another thought.

The guy across the street informed me that two months ago, he and his wife drove up to Michigan to spend some time with his wife's elderly parents. When they returned from their visit, they found that every item of furniture in their house had been moved and rearranged. Everything! Even in the basement! The husband thought that perhaps their adult children had come to their house and had done the deed as a prank, but the kids were just as surprised as the parents were. They called North Canton PD, but really, what could the police do? Nothing had been stolen or damaged in any way, and there was no evidence of forced entry. The police came, looked around, and made a report that was turned over to Detective O'Malley. What else could be done?

Now, here is a curious thing: the folks across the street have told me that, despite the strangeness of their situation, they are actually very pleased with the furniture rearrangement. Not at first, of course, but after a day or two, they came to realize that the interior of their house had been changed for the better. Transformed ~ like magic! There was more free space, for one thing, and the house seemed now to have a more relaxed and friendlier atmosphere as opposed to the previously crowded and basic furniture placement job.

On our side of the street, Sherri has told me that when she discovered that the recliner chair had been moved to the opposite corner of our bedroom, she found that she liked it there. It took a day or two for her to warm up to the change but, yes, she liked it. She said it was the most logical place for the chair to be and how could she not have seen that for herself? Additionally, the dresser had been relocated to the spot where the chair had been. She told me that it almost seemed like a skilled decorator came into the house and moved things around – even though there was absolutely no evidence of heavy moving to be seen in the bedroom or any of the other rooms. No wall scrapes or scratches, no drag marks in the carpeting. Nothing out of the ordinary!

Just off the top of my head, here is an unofficial accounting of mysterious furniture moving incidents (that we know of) in our neighborhood: You already know about our house, and the house directly across the street, which I shall refer to as Neighbor 1. Neighbor 2 reported that everything in the living room and the master bedroom had been rearranged. Further, the bedspread had been changed for a better match with the room color, and they were happy with the results. Also, the TV in the living room had been moved to a more convenient location and the cables were moved and reconnected as well. Neighbor 3 reported that his entire man-cave had been moved, literally moved, to a new location! He also reported that three large, steel cabinets in the garage had been repositioned to make additional parking space available for his new Harley Davidson. He and his wife were very pleased with the changes and, of course, with the new Harley. Neighbor 4 said that everything on his patio and in his sunroom had been moved and intermixed for improved functionality. He also reported that the dining room had also been rearranged. They're very happy as well. Neighbor 5, Mr. Peterson, could not be reached for comment. He was supposedly on the road, delivering household goods to somebody somewhere.

When I next saw Robert Peterson, we were in his rectangular, truck-parking building discussing world events and other generalities, and then I asked him if he had ever experienced anything unusual regarding his furniture or other household items being rearranged and he informed me that he had not. He followed that with, "We have never had that problem, why do you ask?" I told him that I was curious about some unexplained rearranging of furniture in the neighborhood and he smiled; really, it was more like a smirk. I asked him if he and Mrs. Peterson had a pleasant trip and he assured me that, in fact, they did (thus confirming his marital status) followed by another smirk. And then he laughed wickedly, I thought, as he pointed to his moving truck. I looked at the truck but failed to grasp his gesture. What was he trying to tell me? I looked again at the truck, and for the first time, I noticed that the letters on his van didn't say anything like Moving Van, or Peterson's Moving Company, or You Call, We Haul. Instead, I saw that the name of his company was, "I Move Furniture."

"Get it? He said. "No," I said," no idea; what does it mean?" He then explained, "My signage isn't meant to indicate that I move furniture from point A to point B, as most people would take for granted. I did that gig for 23 years." Another smirk now, more of a snarl, I thought. "People just seem to take for granted that because I have a truck, I move their furniture from one place to another, one city to another, one state to another. That's not what I do," he said. "I'm The Moving Man. I move furniture. I just 'move' furniture! I move it this way and that way, or from this spot to that spot." He demonstrated his point by indicating imaginary locations on his garage floor. He said, "Does that make sense to you?" I said, "No it doesn't, but that's just me. Maybe I'm missing something?" He said, "Look, this isn't theoretical nuclear physics here — I 'move' furniture. That's what I do. I am The Moving Man."

What else can I say? Nothing more can be said except that he was still snarling and showing teeth now. And laughing insanely. I backed out of his garage . . . slowly, cautiously and one (large) step at a time.

Press the Button

At 5:45 this morning, someone knocked on my front door. Very loudly, I must say. Can you imagine that? Five forty-five in the morning? They rapped on the door several times, then waited for a response – like I was going to give a response, right? Are you kidding me? Then they rapped a few more times, then again, and again until I had to get out of my bed, throw on a robe and descended to the lower level, all because an unidentified fool was pounding on my door, at 5:45 a.m. Oh yes, I hear you clearly.

I looked out from the bedroom window before going down to the door. I saw nothing of interest in or around our driveway. A person would have to be very reckless not to look out from the window before reacting to early-morning extreme door pounding. As I neared the bottom step, my uninvited visitor was pounding several more times.

When I reached the door, I paused to listen for any tell-tale indications of who the pounder, or perhaps more than one pounder, might be. Someone on the other side of the door said, "Hey, I can hear you breathing. I know you're there." Even though the voice of this pounder was unrecognizable to me, I took a wild and crazy risk and neutralized the security devices, then cautiously pulled the door open to find, on my doormat, a very strange, very large raccoon standing there on its hind legs. The raccoon had an attitude as he stood there on my welcome mat, bracing himself, arms extended with paw pads resting on either side of my doorframe, reminding me of a vertical representation of a man doing a push-up. That's attitude. You just don't lean on someone's door frame at 5:45 a.m.

Now, when I say, "very large," I mean that the raccoon was very large for a raccoon; not very large as in the size of a horse, nothing like that, but big - really big. I'm estimating the height at perhaps four feet, maybe even five feet. That's a big raccoon, I don't care what anybody says.

When the door was fully opened, I told the raccoon to please step back from my door, "don't touch my door," I said. The raccoon replied, "Why should I step back? Are you thinking about attacking me, a vulnerable raccoon? You're going to come out swinging, is that it?" I said, "Please, just step back a few feet. Humor me." The raccoon reluctantly shuffled two or three steps backward, away from the door, then I said, "What could you possibly want with me at 5:45 a.m. Whatever it is, couldn't you have waited until 8 or 9 o'clock?" The raccoon said that he supposed he could have waited but why should he?

See, there it is – that attitude I was talking about. Those damn raccoons all have this smart-ass little attitude, with their eye masks and pointy noses, and those absurd tail rings. The raccoon said, "Your dog has been into my trash again. It's all over West Maple street and I ain't cleaning it up this time." I said, "Okay, fine, don't clean it up, I couldn't care less. And just so you know, my dog isn't even here this week. He's on vacation."

"How convenient," said the raccoon. "Your dog is on vacation while my trash has been dragged all over the street." I said, "You know, this is funny. Exactly how much trash does a raccoon have, anyway? What – some rabbit ribs, eggshells, acorns, seeds? And why would you even *think* about eating a baby rabbit, anyway? And why would my dog bother himself with emptying your trash? Is there something special about your trash that I should know about? I don't think so," I said, defending my dog. "That's not the point!" said the raccoon. "The point is that your dog has been running the streets at night, making noise and raiding trash cans, chasing cars on Woodrow Street, making messes and this behavior has to stop. It's out of control." I was curious as to how this smart-ass, four (maybe five) foot raccoon would even know my dog, "Have you ever actually met my dog?" I asked, "and even if you have met him, how can you be sure that it's my dog and not someone else's dog that happens to look like my dog? What proof do you have – photos? video? Did you actually witness my dog in the act of spilling your trash?"

Of course, we all know it could have been any old dog. I know that and you know that – any old dog, maybe even a dog from another neighborhood, even another county. I told the raccoon that I wasn't going to stand there, at 5:45 a.m. (actually, 6:03 now) arguing with a raccoon. I asked him politely to please go back to his nest or den, or hole, or wherever it is that he calls home. Insulted and discouraged now, he turned and walked away from my porch, then he shouted over his shoulder, "Vacation? That's bullshit!" I replied with a less than sincere, "have a nice day!" He flipped me the paw, then kicked my rose bush on his way to the gate.

So, now I'm wide awake and I'm telling myself that I really need to get this trash can thing under control. Maybe lock the doggie door at night? "Spencer! Spencer, get your butt in here! Right now!" Spencer shouted from his room, "Do you have even the vaguest idea of what time it is?" I shouted back, "So you're going to start with the smart-ass stuff first thing in the morning, right off the bat? Is that how it's going to be?"

"What?!" he said. "You're going to believe that lying raccoon? Everyone knows he's a liar." I said, "Did you do it?" "Yes." he said, "But it's not just me. All the dogs do it. Nobody likes that raccoon." I had to admit that Spencer had a good point there. It's no secret that this raccoon is an agitator and a troublemaker. All the nocturnal animal folks don't like the raccoon. The skunk detests him, every cat in the neighborhood screeches at him, possums hiss at him and show their teeth, he can't go near the streetlights because the bats will attack him (as they should) so he has to sneak around in the shadows all night long. Helluva way to live.

Actually, I was quite surprised to see him lurking on my door-step in the early daylight – like a vampire who has to be back inside the coffin before the sun comes up, and if the vampire doesn't make it in time, his or her head explodes, or whatever it is that happens as punishment to errant vampires in daylight and rebellious raccoons when they have missed a coffin-call. (I'm fairly sure their heads actually blow up, but I could be wrong).

Yet, here he was, in the early light and that might be an indication that maybe he's sick with, you know . . . *rabies*. After all, he did kick my rose bush. And, now that I'm thinking about it, he was leaning rather aggressively against my doorframe. And, I had just realized that he had been *pounding* on the door repeatedly, and not politely, when he had only to ring the damn doorbell. It's 2019 and everyone rings the doorbell. Are we living in 1819, no electricity and all that? He was pounding on the door like a maniac! A very discourteous maniac.

Now what? I'm not going to be the one to call the City Health Department to report a possible rabies case, because that's all it really is – a *possible* case. And I don't want the raccoon to call the dog catcher, in retaliation, the next time he sees Spencer out and about in the neighborhood. And, believe me, this raccoon would make that call! When I verbally pushed the raccoon around this morning, he didn't react like a crazy raccoon, and he wasn't foaming at the mouth, or staggering, or anything like that. True, he was somewhat angry with me, but he didn't behave like a crazed, rabid animal would behave, and he did go peacefully. Well, he did kick the rose bush, but no real damage was done. If the raccoon decides to come back for a repeat performance, it's going to be on him, not me. Rabies or no rabies, I will deal with him accordingly. I do try to be a good neighbor, but this raccoon thing is crossing the line. This is what I must put up with. Raccoons pounding on my door. Geeez!

Things had been peaceful in the neighborhood for a while, then it happened again, the same procedure as the first time, except it wasn't as early. This time it was 7:20 a.m. Loud banging on my door. Thump, Thump, Thump, pause for a minute, Bang, Bang, Bang, and now I'm angry. "Oh, it's go-time, my friend! Oh, It's on!" I said confidently, motivating myself for the coming confrontation. In my entire life, I have never punched a four (maybe five) foot raccoon but today was going to be the day. Yes, I did look out the window, as before, and this time I did see something. There, in my driveway, was a white SUV which I recognized as the vehicle belonging to Impressive David Tuttle.

David lives on Chapel Hill Drive, several blocks from my house and sometimes I see him walking his dog or mowing his grass. I've seen him sometimes at the golf course as well. I dressed hurriedly and went down to the door. Upon opening the door, I saw David holding a dog leash that was attached to the collar around the neck of . . . Spencer.

"What's this all about, David?" I asked. David said, "Well, it's a long story." He handed the leash to me, which I returned to him after putting Spencer in the house. "It was about 6:00 this morning, and I heard the trash can being tipped over and dragged down the driveway. I flipped on the lights and found your dog slinging my trash all over the yard, and my neighbor's yard as well. I knew he was your dog because I've seen you walking with him." I responded, "David, I'm sorry.

I didn't realize that Spencer wasn't in the house. He was here last night, and I assumed that he was here this morning. "David, I'm going to come up there and clean it up for you." David said, "No, that's not necessary. It's already been done. This isn't a really big deal; I just wanted you to know what has happened." I said, "Well, it IS a big deal as far as I'm concerned. I'm sorry about this."

David assured me that all was okay before driving away in his impressive SUV and returning to his impressive house on his impressive tree-lined street where he will dress in his impressive clothes and then go to his impressive job. I don't particularly care for David Tuttle. When he was out of range, I muttered under my breath, "Next time, ring the damn doorbell."

I went into the house and put on the coffee and then I fed Spencer. Neither of us said a word about the "incident" at Impressive David Tuttle's house. Finally, I said, "Spencer, you didn't say anything to him, did you? I mean, you didn't speak, right?"

Spencer assured me that he hadn't said a word to him. So, I said, "What the hell were you thinking? You're lucky that he didn't call the dog catcher." Spencer said, "Yea, that's funny – the dog catcher trying to run – that's hilarious." I said, "How'd you get out? I locked the doggie door." He responded, "I waited until you were asleep, then I nudged the bathroom window up and pushed the screen out. You really shouldn't leave that window partly opened. Somebody could nudge the window up from the outside and come into the house."

During this conversation, I thought I was hearing a muffled sound in the background, possibly originating from the house next door, or maybe from across the street. I heard it, then I didn't hear it. There it was again, slightly louder this time. It sounded like "beep, beep, beep." Then it became louder yet until I found myself waking up, terribly confused, in my bed, as Sherri shook me vigorously. She said, "Is it the bad dream again?" "Ah, Yes." I said. "The usual bad dream." I had to lie about it being "the usual bad dream" because I'm not yet adequately prepared to reveal to her what really goes on inside of my head when I'm sleeping. I have enough on my plate as it is. Baby steps, I think.

I sat up in the bed and stared at the wall until I fully regained my senses. Still hearing, "beep, beep,

beep" I slammed the palm of my hand on the "Off" button of the bedside alarm clock, and the gruesome annoyance mercifully stopped. A glance at the time showed that it was 7:15 a.m. I visually scanned the room, looking for Spencer and found him in his usual spot between the wall and a chair, in front of the closet door. I said, "Spencer, what the hell?" He cocked his head to one side and looked at me, ears arched, with an expression of puzzlement on his face and then I realized that Spencer wasn't going to say anything to me because, well, because dogs can't talk. Once this revelation had settled into my consciousness it also occurred to me that a raccoon can't talk either. That's crazy! A four (perhaps 5) foot raccoon speaking – in English, no less? Ridiculous!

Even though the dream is over, and I have resettled into the normalcy (?) of my world, I'm still trying to put the knocking thing into perspective. I think that it would be nice if people would simply ring a doorbell, if one is available. If the doorbell fails to do the job, or no doorbell is available, we can simply use our cellphones to announce our presence – what a great idea! Really, what's the point of knocking? Door knocking is totally unnecessary, and (I think) very rude. Here in the twenty-first century, we no longer need to knock down the castle drawbridge or pound the hell out of the village gate to make it swing open. Oh, sure, it's always more satisfying to pound on a door. That sort of thing is helpful as a stress reliever in today's high-pressure world, and we know it always gives us that little rush – that false sense of authority and control. But wouldn't it be nice if people would just stop doing stupid shit like pounding their fists on a hard, wooden surface and simply press the little button? I think so. Just press the button!

Yesterday, just to be on the safe side, though not that I thought it was necessary, I nailed the bathroom window closed. If you should find some trash in your yard, or in your driveway, it's not my fault, and even though I always try to be a good neighbor, your trash is not my problem. Don't call me and please don't ever pound on my door.

Press the button.

Mrs. Palmer's Chickens

Yesterday, for the seventh time, I tried to find someone home at Mrs. Palmer's house. As usual, I knocked on her front door. I always knock on her front door because I can't even think about going to the back of her house; it's creepy back there, but as far as I know, the front porch is safe – I think.

Trust me on this, you really don't want to go back there. There are chickens back there. I don't like chickens. I don't trust chickens. Maybe you're okay with chickens, but I'm not.

So, you must be curious about my reason for attempting to visit Mrs. Palmer. I've been trying to offer her my assistance, as Mr. Palmer has recently passed away. Nobody really knows for certain how he died. Mr. Palmer was not much older than sixty, maybe sixty-five at most, and he appeared to have been in good health. Some say that he was crazy and suffered some kind of horrific mental breakdown. Others have said that he died from pneumonia or some type of cancer, while others believe that he most likely drank himself to death. Nobody really knows for sure how Mr. Palmer died because Mr. and Mrs. Palmer always kept to themselves and minded their own business.

The simple reality is that he is dead now and, in his absence, I am attempting to offer help. I can mow the grass, fix the front step, repair the roof, move furniture, whatever I can do to help – that is, whatever I can do that doesn't involve those chickens. I always say, "Never turn your back to a chicken."

I am convinced that Mrs. Palmer is avoiding me. People have told me that she is frequently seen leaving her house in the old, blue, Chevy panel truck, and then returning with groceries and who knows what else. Chicken feed, perhaps? Several times she has been seen rocking on her front porch, reading possibly, or napping. People tell me that Mrs. Palmer always waves at them and exchanges pleasantries. I've seen her occasionally watering her flowers, and from these observations, I conclude that she is in good health and apparently good spirits, considering her unpleasant circumstances, of course. When I see her busying herself with her flowers, I always wave at her, but she never returns my neighborly gesture.

I know when she is at home because I see the old Chevy truck parked under the carport in front of the small garage at the back of the house, next to the chicken coop. So, if I know she's home, she is in the house – maybe avoiding me. I'm trying to be helpful, that's all. Nothing more than that.

Today, for the eighth time, I made another unsuccessful attempt to contact Mrs. Palmer. I rang her doorbell, knocked on the door, and peeked through the small, fan shaped window near the top of the door, which gave me an unobstructed view of her living room. I noticed that the TV was on, and I caught a quick glimpse of her walking around in her kitchen. I know her doorbell works because I could hear the familiar "ding-dong," as I pressed the button several times – and then several more times. I am now considering the possibility that Mrs. Palmer might be deaf. If she isn't deaf, she must be ignoring me. I could have gone to the back of her house, closer to the kitchen, and banged on her back door but quickly decided against that course of action. You know – the chickens.

Someone must feed the chickens, and clean up, and whatever else there is to be done as far as chickens are concerned – eggs and stuff like that. I had decided that perhaps I should wait in my car, up the street, behind her house. Eventually, she will have to come outside, pass under the carport, and follow the walk to the door that leads to inside the coop. My plan was that maybe I could stop her on the pathway to the chicken coop, and explain to her that I am always available in the event that she should need assistance with something around the house –

roof repairs, lawn mowing, stuff like that. I just want to be a good neighbor, that's all.

So, I'm sitting there in my car, a block up the street from Mrs. Palmers chicken coop. I'm waiting to see if Mrs. Palmer will go to the coop, and a North Canton police car rolls up beside my car and the cop flips on the flashing light. A very large cop opened his door and walked around the back of my car, approaching me from the driver side. He shined his flashlight into my face, temporarily blinding me, and asked me if there is a problem with my car. "Are you waiting for roadside assistance?" he asked. I explained that I'm simply watching out for my neighbor's safety because she is a widow and I'm trying to be helpful.

In response to my statement, the very large patrolman informed me that, unfortunately for me, it is *his* job to watch for trouble in the neighborhood and that he doesn't need or want my help. We go through the usual show-me-your-driver-license-and-registration ritual. I gave him what he requested, and he told me to wait there in my car. He then went back to his car and flipped on the interior light. They always flip on that light. I see him talking on his radio.

I'm now sitting, across the table from Detective Sean O'Malley at the police department, and we're talking about coops and chickens and Mrs. Palmer and poor, unfortunate Mr. Palmer, and he asked me why I was sitting in my car, in the dark, at 9:45 at night, behind Mrs. Palmer's house.

I told him that I always keep an eye on my neighbors. The detective then asked me if any *specific* neighbor had ever asked me to keep an eye on him or her (for safety) and now that I'm thinking about it, I realize nobody has ever asked me to keep an eye out for trouble in the neighborhood. The detective then asked me if Mrs. Palmer had asked me to keep an eye on her house. He was very specific in his choice of neighbors; he wanted to know specifically if *Mrs. Palmer* requested that I watch her house. Reluctantly, I told the detective that, no, Mrs. Palmer had never asked for my help in any way. The detective then told me that I was being released, this time, and that if I am again reported by the neighbors for watching over the neighborhood, I would be arrested and charged accordingly.

The detective even went so far as to use finger quotes when he spoke the word, "watching." It appeared to me as though he was implying that I may or may not have been "watching" Mrs. Palmer for reasons other than maintaining a safe neighborhood.

Well, of course, that's just not true, but I wasn't going to argue the details with him at 11:15 on a work night. As I stood to leave the police station, the detective reminded me that the very large police officer will handle the responsibility of watching over the neighborhood. His comment was clearly understood and noted.

Now, please don't misunderstand me here, I am no longer watching out for Mrs. Palmer's safety. I have stayed away from her, as far away as possible, since that last encounter with the very large cop and the unnerving detective. I'm not an idiot. I know when I have failed in a conflict with the police. I have been keeping my verbal commitment to stay out of the neighbors' business and I have come to realize that what I had been doing was over the line – way over! I promise you that I was not "watching" Mrs. Palmer. I was simply watching out for her safety.

That being said, there is no law against me driving past her house on a public street, and I *have* been doing this because, like everyone else, I need to go places and I don't own a helicopter, and I am unable to levitate. So, yes, I drive past Mrs. Palmer's house occasionally.

Mrs. Palmer lives on a corner lot, just off Pittsburg Road, consisting of five acres. Her home, the old family farmhouse, sits on the corner, against two streets. The five acres are mostly on the north side of her house. The remaining acreage of her family's property was sold to developers many years ago. The chicken coop is located on the north side as well, and is accessed by the concrete walk, approximately fifty feet in length.

If one drives past her house on Pittsburg Road running north/south, the back porch of her house cannot be seen. If one drives on the east/west street, however, one can easily see the back porch – and the overgrown grass and the junk and the walk-way leading to the coop and some rusty, old 55-gallon barrels and a lot of other accumulated stuff. On her back porch, there is an old glider, two or three porch chairs and an antique, free-standing coat rack. I'm guessing that this rack is where Mr. Palmer would have hanged his work coat after walking to and from the coop.

Prior to his untimely demise, Mr. Palmer was in the egg selling business – hence the coop and the chickens, and the blue panel truck. On this antique coat rack hangs what appears to be a beekeeper suit, complete with the screened hood, the boots and long gloves. I have never seen (not that I've been looking, mind you) beehives anywhere on the Palmer property. I don't know why the suit hangs there and I don't care – it's none of my business. I never interfere in my neighbors' personal affairs. Ever.

This morning, there was a bit of news which, on the surface, doesn't seem important, but does seem terribly important to *me*. I was sitting in the barber chair at Bell's Barber Shop and two other guys were talking about occasionally seeing Mrs. Palmer going to and from the chicken coup while wearing a beekeepers' suit. (Now do you understand the importance of this news? It's about the chickens!) I'm not sure if these guys were describing the sightings as being recent, or sightings that occurred in the past, but that is irrelevant. What's important here is that she was wearing the suit. She was wearing a beekeeper suit while attending to her chickens. That's weird! That's very disturbing.

It's been two weeks since that informative visit to the barber shop. During all of this time I have had no contact with Mrs. Palmer, and by that, I mean I haven't been (without finger quotes) watching her. As I have told you, I am now leaving police work in the capable hands of the police, where it belongs. I must tell you though, I have driven past her house on the east/west street – the street that affords a view of her back porch – and I have noticed that the beekeeper suit is no longer hanging on the coat rack. It was there a week ago but hasn't been seen since. All this *driving past her house* activity would seem to indicate that I have been making questionable and unnecessary passes on the east/west street – but, I'm not. Really. Just take my word for it, okay?

A day or two has passed since I noticed the absence of the beekeeper suit, and then yesterday, a shock wave passed through not only our neighborhood, but the entire North Canton community as well. Absolute Shock! The entire state of Ohio is in shock. In fact, you might have seen the news coverage on your local TV station no matter where you live!

It seems that Mrs. Palmer was in the habit of wearing the beekeeper suit whenever she went inside the chicken coop to do whatever it is that she did. Mrs. Palmer's sister, Lucille, has told various people that Mrs. Palmer had been wearing the suit lately because the chickens, for some unknown reason, didn't like her. The chickens had no problems with Mr. Palmer, but the chickens always attacked Mrs. Palmer when she entered the coop. The beekeeper suit seemed to give her some small degree of protection from their hostile aggressions. But apparently not enough protection, I'm sorry to say. When the police arrived at the scene, they made a hideous discovery. So hideous, in fact, even the very large patrolman was shaken.

Mrs. Palmer (well, what had once been Mrs. Palmer) was found mangled and literally ripped to small shreds and then partially eaten – only partially eaten because perhaps they didn't have time to finish her off and pick her bones prior to the discovery of the "crime" scene. There was no evidence to suggest that something other than chickens had done the deed. No coyotes or bears or foxes are suspected. Based on Mrs. Palmer's wounds, all evidence points to the chickens, and based on the undeniable fact that blood stains were found on every chicken in the coop. Not random blood smears here and there, rather, a literal bloodbath of evidence was found on every single bird, as well as the blood on the walls and parts of the ceiling. To make matters worse, the coroner reported that the slaughter had occurred about three or four days prior to discovery of the body.

I don't care what anybody says, that's one hell of a terrible way to go out of this world. I can think of only one worse way to go, and that is to be ground up, while alive, in a tree and stump-grinding machine.

During the course of the investigation, the police also found hundreds of chicken carcasses literally packed into the 55-gallon barrels – crammed to the top rim of each barrel and covered with old newspapers and then sealed with the rusty lids which had been weighted down with bricks and stones to prevent the wind from blowing the lids off and exposing the evidence.

The police also reported that there was no chicken food to be found anywhere inside or outside of the coop. The house was also thoroughly searched for chicken food with zero results. Nothing in the carport or the blue truck, or the small garage either. This would indicate that efforts were being made to deliberately starve the chickens.

I guess the chickens had enough of Mrs. Palmer, both figuratively and literally.

Remember, never turn your back to a chicken.

The Glory Days

This is what I have heard various people say about the Glory Days:

"I remember my glory days like those days were yesterday."

"Those glory days were the best days of my life."

"Sometimes I wish I could magically go back there and re-live some of those days."

"I occasionally entertain myself by imagining that I could simply close my eyes and choose a specific memory, and when my eyes reopen, I would actually be there – not just in my mind, but in my physical body as well. Wouldn't that be incredible?"

(yawn)

The problem I have with all of this is that I am unable to distinguish which days, if any, might have been my glory days and which days were not. I now have 27,375 days behind me, and I can recall only about twenty-five percent of that number – ok, if I'm honest, maybe only ten percent. Most of my days were, to be truthful, not that great. They weren't terrible days, or bad days, but they weren't glory days either – just ordinary, unremarkable days. Who decides which days are the glory days? That's what we need to talk about.

Now, here is the setback: What if, by this point in my life, I haven't experienced any of my allotted glory days? I don't have an answer for this question because, as far as I know, we don't know that we are experiencing a glory day, even when the glory is supposedly happening to us. I think when we experience a good day, or an exceptionally good day, or perhaps a really, really great day, we don't think of this particular day as a glory day until looking back, later in life. We make a mental note about that day, perhaps, but we don't think of the day as being glory-worthy until later when we need something glorious to think about.

I don't think I've ever said to myself, "Wow, I think I just might have had a glory day! I am going to record this day in my little blue book so I will have a permanent record of that day, and I can look back to that day any time I feel the need to do so." I don't know why anyone would want to do that, but, okay – whatever works for you.

What if we had never been allotted glory days – in other words, what if there really is no such thing as glory days and the entire glory day concept was nothing more than a poorly-conceived idea from day one? Or worse, an outright lie—a total con job. What if we only imagined that we had experienced a glory day because we have learned to expect that we are somehow entitled to our *anticipated* glory days. Did we simply declare our own glory days based on our own egos?

We like to think that we've all had glory days, but if you think about it, the only times we ever hear the words, "Glory Days" used openly, these words are usually spoken in an athletic, or musical, or academic context. People will say things like, "Yep, Old Billy Jones was a helluva football player back in his college glory days!"

However, these glory day lookbacks, if you think about it, are actually more negative and less positive because it is *implied* here that Old Billy Jones hasn't done anything else with his life after chasing a football for four years. We must now assume that the rest of Old Billy's days were just ordinary, ho-hum days. Billy had apparently been allotted only four years of glory and we know that in the grand scheme of things, four years of football isn't the only glory-worthy thing to have lived for. Well, for most people it isn't.

The above scenario can also be applied to the entertainment industry—for example, musical groups, some of which we don't/can't even remember anymore. We might hear someone say, "Oh hell yea, I remember *that* group! Back in their glory days it was nearly impossible to get tickets for their concerts!" Fifty-five years later, though, nobody cares anymore because most of us have come to our big boy/big girl realizations that maybe that band, back in the band's glory days, wasn't as great as we had imagined it was when we're judging using the perspective of a frontal cortex brain that had not yet been fully developed.

Occasionally, we can observe the results of this "not fully developed brain" phenomenon when we occasionally spot that ever-popular, fifty-year-old guy slamming the imaginary strings on his imaginary "air guitar" reliving his supposed glory days at a Tuba Skinny concert on the sidewalk in New Orleans.

While there is an *acoustic* guitar player and a banjo player in the group, they're not swinging their string-pickin' arms wildly in a semicircle above their head and then downward, like a goose trying to become airborne with a broken wing. That's just a sad example of a fifty-year old guy trying desperately to re-live his <u>imagined</u> glory days as a rock-star *impersonator*. That guy is still out there somewhere! He's having fun, but, really, do we have to watch this spectacle every time this guy has had a couple of beers when someone is playing music?

Another prime example of a person's supposed glory days would be our esteemed politicians. We've all heard about this politician's or that politician's glory days.

You know what? I have just realized that I can't think of any politician having glory days to reflect upon.

Let's consider the effect of glory day accumulation for those individuals who have dedicated their lives to the pursuit of knowledge. The PhDer's, the astronomers, the inventors, the mathematicians, imaginative theoretical physicists and so forth. There is no way, that I can think of, to compensate these people by bestowing the ever-elusive glory days upon them I can honestly say that I've never heard anyone say, "Hey, how about that Einstein fella and his theory of relativity? The guy's a genius! Yessir, back in Albert's glory days, he was really something!" So, when, exactly, did Albert's glory days begin and when did they end? Are we to believe that Albert hypothesized his relativity theory and then stopped working because he knew that someday soon, people would be talking about his glory days, and then he could relax and do crossword puzzles for the next forty years?

Or, consider Isaac Newton. Without Isaac, apples might fall side-ways and we would all be wearing steel boots to help us stay grounded. Thank you, Isaac. We all love you, Isaac, but you can't have glory days because nobody knew about glory days back in the sixteenth century. Or the seventeenth century, or the eighteenth century, and we're not sure about the nineteenth either. We don't know when glory days were discovered and then forced upon us. I'm not going to carry these academic examples any further here because, as I have said, "I don't think the people in this category would care one way or the other.

Maybe I'm following the wrong path here. Perhaps I wasn't paying attention to the map and I took a wrong turn. I'm sure I took a wrong turn. Somewhere between the rock star *impersonator,* and the politicians, I concluded that it's probably time to look at this whole glory days thing from a fresh perspective – new eyes, so to speak.

I'm going to abandon the term, "Glory Days" and banish it from my personal vocabulary, forever. Do we really need to hold on to this choice of words? I think some people will, unfortunately, never have glory days to look back on and this is very disturbing. Right now, as we are engaging ourselves in this story, there are people out there feeling unworthy of the designation of having lived such glory days. Perhaps these people were not blessed with athletic abilities, or musical abilities, or academic abilities and these people are trying to understand why they haven't been granted glory days; they are most likely feeling undervalued and therefor rejected.

Sorry—you didn't qualify so you can't have glory days to look back on.

Really, what are the criteria for a time to qualify as one's glory days anyways? How does one know if they qualify for the special privilege of having glory days to look back on? I suggest we simply replace the term "Glory Days" with the phrase "Good Life." That's really what the glory days are all about, and it makes so much more sense to look back on our life and say something like, "I have had a good life. I gave it my best shot, I tried to the best of my ability, and I feel pretty damn good about that." One could say, "All of my days were good days, and I feel pretty damn good about that."

Going back to Old Billy Jones, we could say, "You know? I feel sorry for Old Billy Jones. I just do. What a shame that Old Billy only got notoriety for four years of chasing a football."

Truthfully, I've had a damn good life and every day of my life was pretty damn good and I don't need special glory day recognition for anything I have done or may not have done.

Here's what you need to remember, my friends – Just give it your best shot and call it a day. When the bus stops, it's time to get off. What more can I say? Glory days be damned.

Lighten up. Treat yourself (below) to some fun. Life is good – enjoy it. No matter what.

https://www.youtube.com/watch?v=904BN6HW1RI

Ghosts

Usually I don't give personal advice, but I will make a rare exception in this case because I'm thinking that maybe I can help you — or maybe not, but that is for you, the reader, to determine, I suppose.

I want to share what I have learned in the school of life: Being polite is bullshit if you are being polite out of a misdirected sense of obligation to make people like you. Sometimes, let's be honest, most times, you will be better off if you simply keep your mouth closed and mind your own business while the people around you enthusiastically humiliate themselves as they go about expressing their foolishness as fact. If you avoid their foolish conversations, you avoid the social consequences of arguing with a fool. Be a good listener but keep your thoughts to yourself and recognize these foolish people for who they really are — teachers of what not to do when a conversation begins to run wildly out of control. Smile and nod your head occasionally to indicate your attentiveness to their comments but keep your thoughts private. Once they have formed their opinions, they will never agree with yours, anyway.

If you are thirty-something as you are reading this, it's most likely your opinion of my advice will not be the same opinion you will have at say, age sixty-something.

Case in point, until a month ago, I was an unwavering non-believer in ghosts. When I was a youngster, I wanted to believe; I tried my very best to believe, but I couldn't get past this haunting thing which was the only roadblock on my journey to full acceptance. I asked myself, "If there are ghosts, why would they choose to hang around, for decades or centuries, in such places as a dark basement or an old cemetery, deeply concealed in the backyard shadows or in a dark bedroom closet?" There are so many more positive things for ghosts to do with their limitless spare time; so many places for them to go visit that they missed in their earthly lifetimes, instead of them hanging around in unexciting places, making mischief and terrifying kids.

We have friends who are absolutely convinced that a ghost is living in their home. They claim it is semi-solid — not merely a shadow on the wall. It has been seen many times in various spaces throughout the house, and occasionally out of doors as well. They say that the family dog also can see it and occasionally interacts with it.

It started on the day they were moving from their starter home, into their forever home. The Misses had been carrying boxes from the tailgate of the rental truck that had been backed into the driveway and parked about twenty feet from the garage door. She was stacking the boxes in the garage, beside the door that led from the garage to the basement stairs or the kitchen, depending on which direction you turned upon entering the house. She grabbed another carton from the tailgate and as she turned toward the garage, she was shocked to see a man casually walking through the door and into her house. The man entered and turned to his right, which would have sent him to the basement. Her first thought was that perhaps this man was a friend of her husband, possibly coming to help with the move.

After carrying the carton into the garage, she set it on top of the others and went into the house to say, "Hello" to the man. Except that there was nobody on the basement steps or in the kitchen. She went down to the basement and looked everywhere for the man but there was nobody there. Thinking that the man had gone the other way, through the kitchen and further into the house, she looked everywhere upstairs but found nobody. She found her husband in the master bedroom, busily assembling the bedframe and headboard. She told him about the man she had seen entering the house. She described the man to her husband, from his red hair atop his head, his slender build and approximate height of 6 feet, and that he was wearing Khaki trousers, leather shoes and a white, long-sleeve shirt, open at the collar. She and her husband searched the house thoroughly and found no trace of the person fitting her description. Neither did they see a car in or near the driveway. This was the only time this solid man has been seen. All other unusual sightings of the ghostly type have been of the semi-solid variety.

I know another person who is convinced that he is being visited by dead people. He claims that his situation isn't especially frightening, and he views these visits as mildly annoying and sometimes embarrassing when the unexpected visits occur in public places.

He began giving me an example of a recent public incident. "I was walking to no particular place in the mall when I saw two people approaching me from a distance. As these people drew nearer, eventually entering my personal space, I realized that these people were my relatives, Aunt Beverly and Uncle Robert. The same Beverly and Robert who died about eighteen years ago." He told me that his Uncle Robert passed first, in 2002 and then Beverly passed in 2006.

Not only did his deceased aunt and uncle approach him, but his aunt even gave him a hug. His Uncle Robert, who was never one for affection, seemed to just keep checking his watch, as if he was keeping them on a schedule.

He noticed Robert's obvious lack of interest and remembered that, for some obscure reason, Robert never really liked him, and his feelings toward Uncle Robert were quite the same. On the other hand, Beverly was absolutely thrilled to see him, and she was beaming with unchecked enthusiasm.

His aunt then started talking to him, asking how his mother was. Given that he was now conversing with a ghost, he found himself wanting to go along with the conversation, just long enough to watch this train run off the track.

He sarcastically replied to Beverly, "Ahh, she's dead?" Beverly was shocked. "Oh no! When did she go?" He responded, "Ahh, about thirty-four years ago?" "Oh my! She said, I'm so sorry to hear that. What happened?" Mockingly, he repeated, "Ahh–she died?" His aunt looked at him with a strange expression, took a small step backward and disappeared instantly. "Poof! She was gone!" He said. (Actually, he described it as more like a "popping" sound). Then his Uncle Robert said, "Well, gotta go now. Good to see ya. Take care." Another "pop" and

Uncle Robert was gone as well. He said it was like watching a balloon explode six inches in front of his face.

He explained that it felt like a perfectly normal interaction, outside of the fact that he was conversing with dead people, and he did notice that other folks in the mall seemed to be looking at him with curiosity and going out of their way to avoid him.

Totally normal.

Last Sunday night, after pondering these examples of ghostly interactions, I decided that I would intentionally make myself vulnerable to the unknown — the supernatural, ghostly entities that might be lurking about — and see what, if anything, might happen to me. I know this is peculiar activity for a man of my age, but I am a ghost skeptic and I will take extraordinary measures to demonstrate my point.

I had decided that I would begin the experiment after the 11:00 evening news and continue with my research project through the night until dawn — usually around 5:30 a.m. at this time of year. I am, of course, aware that ghosts can and will occasionally make themselves available during the daylight hours as well, but where's the fun in that? I say, "If you're going to do something big, do it to the best of your ability." If necessary, I can always repeat this experiment at some other time, perhaps during the daylight hours. Probably not, though.

I made a plan based on a typical summertime, six-hour night—11:00 p.m. to 5:30 a.m., give or take a few minutes either way. I broke the activities down into three categories of locations at which to experience a ghostly phenomenon: Cemetery, Backyard Shadows, and Bedroom Closet.

The Cemetery: I wanted to get this obvious location out of the way early, before the nighttime chill, set in — this is Ohio, after all. Also, if I left our house at 10:30 p.m., I would have enough time to stop at the ice cream parlor and pick up a small dish of peanut butter/chocolate fudge. The cemetery is no more than a ten-minute drive from the parlor, so I would arrive at the cemetery at around 10:50 p.m., giving me ten minutes to enjoy my ice cream before going on duty as a ghost detector

When I arrived at the north cemetery gate on Orion Road, it was locked. I hadn't anticipated this unfortunate setback. I turned around and went to the west gate on Pittsburg Road and was equally disappointed there as well. I probably should have thought this project through before committing to a whimsical, poorly planned experiment such as this. I returned to the north gate and parked across the street from the cemetery, in the parking lot of a dog grooming shop that had been torn down to make room for a planned, future round-about at this intersection.

I walked across the street and into the cemetery where I followed the path to the older graves, where the trees are older too. I found a tree close to the path and I sat on the ground, using the tree as a backrest. After thirty minutes of detecting (nothing) and observing, I decided to move a little further back, eventually finding myself in an area where the gravestones were showing dates from the 1800's. I walked around this section for a while, not feeling like I was accomplishing anything worthwhile. In my opinion, this part of my experiment should be considered as nothing more than time not well-spent. I did, however, detect and observe a large, shaggy dog wandering around for a few minutes, lifting his leg occasionally at his favorite gravestones, eventually heading for the wooded area at the edge of the graveyard, not to be seen again. Possibly the dog was actually a ghost revealing itself as a dog? You never know. A good ghost observer must consider all possibilities. Here is my takeaway from this experience: If I were a ghost, I wouldn't waste my time hanging around in a cemetery. What's the point of that? Even a shaggy old dog doesn't waste much time in a cemetery. I pronounced this part of the experiment dead at 12:45 a.m.

The Backyard Shadows: A little after 1:00 in the morning, I returned to our house and parked in the driveway because I didn't want to disturb my wife as I worked on parts 2 and 3 of the Great Ghost Experiment. I had decided on the way home from the cemetery that I would detect and observe ghostly activity in the backyard shadows first, then the bedroom closet would be investigated last. I closed the car door very softly so as not to disturb my wife or our neighbors. I went around the house to a gate that separates the backyard from the rest of the lot. I opened the gate as quietly as possible and when I stepped into the backyard, the security floodlights were activated (Several lights, actually, since one can never be too careful when securing one's home) bathing me in a brilliant field of bone-penetrating white light. This disturbed (embarrassed) me and I was forced to conclude at this point that if there were any ghosts there in the shadows, the light would surely have frightened them away — or perhaps dissolved them like sulfuric acid poured on a porkchop. Again, I admit this entire debacle was a poorly planned and a carelessly executed project from the beginning. "I can fix this, though," I thought to myself.

With a positive attitude, I returned to the driveway where I noticed the interior light inside my car was on, which reminded me that I had intentionally failed to close the driver-side door solidly. I made a mental note to take care of this condition later before going to the closet to continue my ghost detection experiment, and then proceeded to the keypad on the exterior wall, beside our garage door. I pressed the numbers of my super-secret code into the keypad and watched as the door began its upward journey, then stopping the door as it reached the 3-foot mark off the ground. I didn't want the door motor to run any longer than necessary because this probably would have created a very serious problem for me if I had awakened my sleeping wife. Like a garage Ninja, I rolled under the bottom edge of the door, then kind of jumped up and limped directly to the security control panel where I flipped the backyard floodlight switch to the "off" position. Then, I Ninja rolled back out of the garage and then returned to the darkened backyard.

I went to our back porch and obtained a chair that I carried to the approximate center of the yard, where I had planned to sit. There I waited. And waited. I moved the chair a little deeper into the yard, closer to the back fence. And then, having sat there for about forty-five minutes, I saw something! It was absolutely thrilling! Something was moving away from the side fence and coming closer to my location. Holy shit! Something dark and menacing was in the yard, moving and stopping, slithering and occasionally . . . hopping. I waited until the rabbit had crossed the yard, then called off the ghost detecting and observing at this location around 2 in the morning. Part 2 completed.

The Bedroom Closet: Every kid, at one time or another, has had this unfortunate ghostly experience. Every parent, at one time or another, has opened the closet door and invited the kids to see for themselves that the closet is empty. It's always empty, but everyone knows the ghost is still in there, hiding, jeering, taunting — this is what ghosts do. I crept into the bedroom walk-in closet and carefully pulled the door closed behind me, immediately regretting that I had forgotten to bring a stool for the closet. And I had forgotten to bring a flashlight as well. These items could have/should have been pre-located had I been properly prepared for this "adventure gone terribly wrong." Even the Boy Scouts know about being prepared. I would have to sit on the closet floor and feel my way around as I went about the business of waiting for the closet ghost to make his or her appearance: all of this hopefully without startling my wife, who was sleeping soundly, laying diagonally across both her and my sides of the bed.

After an hour or so of uncomfortable darkness, not to mention stuffiness, I became bored with this experiment and decided this would be the perfect time to have some fun, if nothing else. I decided that I would tap lightly several times on the closet wall. I tapped and waited for a response which did not come.

I waited another minute or two and tapped again, "Come to bed. What are you doing in there?" my wife asked to the dark room. I, of course, did not respond to her inquiry. As far as I know, ghosts are not required to explain what they're doing — I don't know how or why, but this seems to be the case and who am I to dispute that rule? I don't write the guidelines. I tapped again, twice on the wall. "Stop it! I was asleep!" my wife retorted. I waited for five minutes and pounded a little louder which started our dogs barking at 3:00 a.m.

I heard her scrambling out of the bed and across the floor toward the closet door. She pulled the door open and flipped on the light switch. "Okay! That's enough! Come to bed or sleep on the couch." The dogs were still barking. I flipped off the closet light switch and bailed out of the closet. Part 3 not completed, and nor will it ever be completed.

The following morning, I went outside to get the newspaper from the driveway, and I noticed that I had forgotten to close the garage door during the night-time events. I used the exterior keypad to fully open the garage door and then stepped into the garage just in time to see a possum scrambling from the back of the garage toward the open door, and freedom. When I attempted to start my car, of course the battery was dead. I did make a mental note the night before as a reminder to slam the door solidly, making sure the interior light was off. Unfortunately, I had forgotten about the mental note and now the car wasn't going to start. We have jumper cables, but that's not the point.

Was the experiment worth it? In a word — NO. Well, maybe Yes if we consider that I was able to score a small peanut butter/chocolate fudge ice cream — that's a positive, right? So, what have we learned from this experience? Absolutely nothing that we didn't already know from a lifetime of our own weird experiences. Things go bump in the night; that's the nature of a home. There is always a sensible answer, and there are always ridiculous answers. I think we tend to gravitate toward the ridiculous ones. Admit it, we all do it. We see a shadow on the wall and, of course, it must be a ghost. Or, a portrait that had been hanging above the fireplace mantle falls from the wall and crashes on the floor, both examples surely the work of an annoying spirit? Never mind that the nail which had been holding the portrait to the wall had loosened and finally slipped out of the wall after years of traffic vibrations from a nearby street. It happens.

Matthew and Julianne Collins

Part 1: Matthew

Matthew Collins and his charming wife, Julianne, were married in September 2005. The happy couple moved into their Cape Cod house on Spring Valley Road almost exactly two years from the date of their wedding. Matt and Juli were two very determined people and, as such, they took their declared life-plan very seriously. During the two-year period between the wedding and the purchase of their forever home high above the valley, they lived in a small one-bedroom apartment closer to the downtown area where there wasn't much of a view, unless you appreciated concrete and slow-moving traffic.

They had seen a lovely Cape Cod home one day while driving to nowhere in particular and they decided that someday they were going to have a Cape Cod exactly like that one. The house of their dreams would have white, clapboard cedar siding, gray roof shingles and dark, moss-green shutters. The house would sit on no less than a half-acre in a quiet neighborhood where stately trees attracted birds and squirrels and blocked out the intense afternoon sun.

Matthew worked out of his home-office as a sales representative for an industrial supply company. Julianne was a pharmacist at one of the two local hospitals. Her job required that she rotate shifts between days and afternoons. Every other week, Matthew was required to attend a sales meeting at his company's headquarters, which was an hour drive each way. As scheduled, once a month, Juli enjoyed a long, four-day weekend during which they would take occasional short trips to auctions or flea markets in the surrounding area or tend to the garden and manicured yard. Every evening, weather permitting, they enjoyed their spacious patio which overlooked the twinkling lights below in the valley. Some evenings they stayed longer on the patio to watch the occasional shooting star displays. Life on Spring Valley Road was good; one could even say it was perfect.

Two weeks ago, on a Tuesday, Julianne did not come home on time from the hospital after completing her afternoon shift which concluded at 10:30 p.m. This was not unusual, as she was sometimes in the habit of stopping occasionally at the nearby convenient store on her way home to pick something up or fill her tank. Matthew wasn't overly concerned. He watched the 11 o'clock news and weather report as usual and decided that he would go to bed before Juli got home, which was also not uncommon because he made his sales calls early in the mornings. After lying in bed for about twenty minutes, Matthew was anxious and unable to fall asleep. He was concerned about the whereabouts of Juli. It was nearly midnight now, and he had an uneasy feeling that he couldn't shake off.

Matthew called Juli but she wasn't answering. He also tried texting her, with no results. He repeated this process two more times, with Juli never answering The pharmacy was closed at that hour, so he called the special outside line and spoke to the security guard Jason, who explained that he hadn't seen Julianne when he passed by the pharmacy earlier in the evening. Nor did he see her as she passed by his post while on her way to the parking lot. Hearing the concern in Matthew's voice, Jason tried to assure Matthew that just because he hadn't actually seen Julianne, it didn't necessarily mean that she wasn't in either of these two places. It simply meant that he didn't *see* her there, in the pharmacy, or leaving the hospital. Jason said he would "take a look around" and call Matthew back. Jason called at 12:40 a.m.to inform Matthew that, according to several people, Julianne did, in fact, complete her shift and that her car was not in her usual parking spot. Further, Jason said that he drove around the perimeter of the hospital property thinking that he might find Julianne and/or her disabled car somewhere other than on hospital property but found nothing out of the ordinary.

Matthew thanked Jason and hurriedly dressed and backed his car out of the garage with the intention of searching the area around her route for an hour or so and if he didn't find Julianne, he would then call the police. After an hour of driving aimlessly through the neighborhood and backtracking the route to and from the hospital, Matthew gave up and called the police. He was informed that the police would not get involved in a case such as this one for at least 24-hours unless foul-play was suspected. Nevertheless, Detective O'Malley called Matthew about an hour later, inviting him to "Come down to the station and we can have a talk." Matthew responded, "I have no problem with that, but are we going to actually look for her or are we going to talk and then wait for twenty-two more hours?" O'Malley, being a man of few words, merely said, "Just come down and we'll talk."

Matthew arrived at the police station visitor parking area twenty minutes later with an attitude. He was tired and anxious and incredulous about the fact that his wife was obviously missing but apparently not officially missing yet, in the words of the police. After parking, he followed the yellow arrows meticulously stenciled on the sidewalk to the visitor entrance where he was buzzed-in by Detective O'Malley.

"Coffee?'" asked the detective. "No," Matt, angrily responded. O'Malley led Matthew down a hall that opened into a darkened office area which was deserted at this hour. "Right this way," O'Malley said, extending his arm toward the open door leading to an interview room. "You're sure you don't want some coffee? We don't charge for coffee." Matthew didn't find the intended humor in the cop's query. "No. No thanks. Sorry, I don't drink coffee, it makes my heart pound." "Yea, me too." Said O'Malley. "I'm probably crazy but I drink it anyway because it's always here. It's either going to be coffee or lukewarm drinking fountain water that smells like sulfur."

Sean O'Malley was a clever investigator. Sean O'Malley was also a good-old-boy, or a loud-mouth slob, or a strong, silent caregiver, or whatever character was called for at any given moment. In this particular case, though, O'Malley was operating in "kindly, concerned father" mode, skillfully handling Matthew, who was naively thinking to himself that he could school this detective in a thing or two. Matthew lived a sheltered life as a kid, and as an adult as well. He absolutely was not equipped to play in the big league with this very large and skillful Irish cop. Sean O'Malley was in his happy place. He smiled, opened a fresh legal pad and placed it on the table-top, clicked his pen and began the interview.

"So, let's just cut to the chase, here. Tell me what *you* think might have happened, if anything. Where do you think your wife is?" Matthew was a bit shaken, he wasn't expecting an accusing gut punch, so he was defensive as he exclaimed, "Hey! *I* called *you*! Are you suggesting that I had something to do with this?" O'Malley simply asked, "**Did** you **do** something? I'm just asking you a very simple question." Matthew pushed his chair away from the table and stood to . . . what? What did he think he was going to do?

O'Malley said, "Matthew, sit down. I'm trying to rule you out, but you're not helping me. If you didn't do anything, then what do you think happened?" Matthew said, "We don't know that anything has happened." O'Malley replied, "Ok, so, tell me what you're thinking." Matthew told O'Malley that if he had an idea about where Julianne might be, he wouldn't have called the police in the first place.

O'Malley pressed him again. "Look, this is the part I hate most about these things, but I have to ask; Is your marriage in a good place? No accusations here, I'm just trying to cover all the bases." Matthew, a bit deflated, said, "I get it. You're doing your job. No! I don't suspect anything like… that. Never." O'Malley responded, "Okay. We can move away from this question, but to be clear, you ARE telling me that you are sure things are all good, correct?" Matthew said, "I'm telling you that she isn't involved in anything like what you're insinuating – our marriage is great. Things are all good."

O'Malley said, "What about friends? Does your wife have close friends? Friends that she would spend time with? At 2:00 in the morning? Without giving you a heads-up?" Matthew told the detective that, yes, Julianne did have a close friend but that she would never go anywhere after working the afternoon shift—other than the occasional convenient store or gas station stop before heading straight to their home. He further explained that Julianne's friend, Debra, rises very early for work because she has a 6:00 a.m. start time at a small business that is located twenty miles from her home. O'Malley said, "Good to know. I think I'll have a patrol officer drive out there and have a look-see. Do you have the address?" Matthew told O'Malley that Debra lived on Woodrow Street as he fumbled through his phone to find the address. "It's 136 Woodrow," he said, "But, Julianne won't be there."

O'Malley pushed his chair away from the table and went to the dispatch console where he asked the officer on duty to send a car to 136 Woodrow to look around for Juliann's vehicle—a white Subaru Outback.

The detective returned to the interview room. "Are you sure you don't want something to drink? I can raid the secretary's desk drawer and see if I can find you a decaf tea bag. Will that work?" Matthew declined. Sean knew that Matthew would refuse the offer, but what else could he do to irritate Matthew at 2:30 a.m. that he hadn't already done?

The patrol officer called in on his radio to inform all listening that he had checked the house and did not find a white Subaru Outback outside or inside the garage. In the garage was a Red VW registered to Debra Clark. Additionally, there was a Chevy Pickup truck parked in the driveway, registered to Roger Clark. The hood was cool to the touch and there was moisture forming on the windshield, indicating that the truck, most likely, had not been recently driven. The house was dark. The officer also checked the backyard and found nothing of interest. Having done these things, the officer cleared the call and left the area.

Even though the police would not open an official missing person investigation until twenty-four hours had passed, patrol personnel had been informed of the license plate number and a description of Julianne's vehicle. The police were on the lookout, but there was no sign of Julianne or her vehicle.

Part 2: Julianne

Julianne said goodnight to her coworkers, "See you guys tomorrow," she said. Bill Miller threw a paper ball at her as she passed him in the hallway on her way to the door. "Later!" Bill called out to her, following with his standard line, "Be safe out there!" Just before she pushed the lock-bar on the door and stepped into the not exactly warm but not exactly cool night air, a discomforting feeling settled upon her like a wet blanket. Not a heavy, immediately threatening sensation, though. It was more like a "something isn't right" kind of thing. A feeling of being watched, perhaps, but she knew this anxiety would soon pass; it always did. She has had this feeling many times before. The season was changing and Juli was looking forward to a Saturday afternoon of college football and heavy snacking. Thinking of the game and her living room occupied her mind and relieved her apprehension somewhat.

Jason wasn't in the security office as she passed by on her way to the parking lot, but this wasn't unusual for Jason. He had varied responsibilities and couldn't always sit in the office to wave at the employees as they passed by. He was busy fellow. Julianne went directly to her car, started the engine and pulled out of her spot and then out of the parking lot, heading East on Chapel Hill, her favorite radio station abusing her eardrums. Julianne locked her doors. Bad Mojo. Something wasn't right.

At this time of night, there were very few, if any, cars travelling toward Juli in the opposite lane. Nobody living in the upper mountain area would be driving towards the city now. Likewise, few people were going upwards into the mountains this time of night. As Juli rounded a corner, she saw the lights at the convenient store in the distance, to her left. The lights seemed to be surrounded by rings of fine mist and she noticed that her windshield was collecting a fine coating of mist as well. As Juli drew nearer to the store, she remembered that she needed to pick up some Ginger Ale—her favorite downtime beverage.

She pulled onto the lot and parked close to store, right in front of the front door. Passing the nighttime clerk, Eric, at the counter, she went straight to the coolers against the back wall—milk, coffee creamer, and ice cream in the right side. Beer, soft drinks and bottled water in the left side. As she was moving toward the counter, billfold and Ginger Ale in hand, she grabbed a bag of chips thinking that she might watch a movie before going to bed and she remembered that she needed to get her phone on the charger—soon. "How's Juli tonight?" Eric said, breaking into her thoughts. She responded, "Hey, Eric, what's new with you?" Eric told Julianne that he was feeling gloomy. He didn't want to see cold weather coming so soon and Juli agreed, "Yea, who needs this, right?" Eric asked if she needed a bag for the chips. She told him that she would be working on the chips as she drove, but thanks anyway. "See ya later," Eric called out as Juli passed through the door and into the cold, night drizzle.

Julianne had about ten more minutes left in her trip home when she felt the sudden, frightening vibrations coming through the steering wheel and into her forearms. Within seconds, she was barely able to control the car and she had no choice but to pull over onto the shoulder. Luckily, she was able to maintain control of her car until she had the vehicle fully stopped. Prior to stepping outside to assess the damage to her right-front tire, she instinctively checked her rear-view mirror even though she was sure there were no other cars anywhere nearby. There were no other cars in sight, but she did notice a misty illumination in the distance. Within a few seconds it became obvious to her that she was now looking at two headlights which she estimated to be about a quarter of a mile away.

She returned to the driver-side and re-entered the car. She switched on the emergency flashers, locked the doors and waited while the car approached as she watched the progress in the rearview mirror. She noted that the car was moving to the opposite lane in an effort to pass by, indicating that the driver had no intention of stopping to give assistance, and this disturbed her and comforted her at the same time. She was comforted because she had a very bad case of the jitters, and simultaneously annoyed because what kind of person would not think to at least check on the driver—just in case the stranded driver might be seriously ill. "People are so inconsiderate," she thought. She attempted to call Matthew, but the phone was dead. She saw the small message at the top of the screen indicating that the battery charge was less than one percent. Not even enough power to make one call. Juli had a charger for her phone but it was on her kitchen counter.

As she sat there, on the shoulder, looking forward while in deep consideration of her situation, she noticed that the car which had just passed by had pulled over onto the shoulder about two-hundred yards in front of her, and it was slowly moving backwards toward her car. She immediately thought,

"Well, what do you know, someone had a change of heart and is coming back to help me." Her next thought was, "What if this person isn't planning to help, but maybe do something else?" Her first impulse was to run, but where would she go? The car was getting closer now as it slowly approached in reverse. Close enough now that she could see only one person in the car. She went into her purse and grabbed her pepper spray, holding it tightly now as she awaited the car's arrival. The car stopped ten feet from Juli's front bumper, and the driver turned on the emergency flashers. The driver exited his car and walked toward Juli's side window while motioning for her to roll the window down.

Julianne had no intention of lowering her window, instead she showed the pepper spray to the man. The man ordered her again to lower the window and she flipped him the bird. He smiled and reached inside of his jacket to get, what now, a gun? He extracted his badge case and flipped it open for her inspection while explaining that he was an off-duty police officer. She flipped the bird again. The off-duty cop said, "Okay, just lower your window an inch so we can talk and pop your trunk open. Do you have a useable spare?" Julianne said, "As far as I know, the tire is good." She opened her window a half-inch and pulled the trunk release. The cop said,

"Mrs. Collins, I'm going to jack your car upward and change your tire. Please do not exit your car for your safety and mine." Julianne said, "How do you know my name is Collins?" The cop explained that he had called in her license plate number as he passed her car. He further explained that he had planned to call a tow truck for her but decided against that course of action because he wasn't sure how long that service call would have taken at that late hour.

After completing the tire change, which took no longer than perhaps fifteen minutes, the cop told Juli that her husband was on his way there as they spoke. "Would you like for me to stay with you until his arrival?" he asked her. Juli said, "No thank you, I only have a five-minute drive from here. I'll be fine. Thank you, though, for your assistance." They both laughed as the cop flipped her the finger as he said, "You're very welcome."

Julianne sat there for a minute or two waiting to assure herself that the cop did, in fact, go away. When she was satisfied that the officer was gone, she started her car with the intension of checking her mirror as she always did when pulling into moving traffic. Not expecting to actually see an approaching car at this late hour, she carelessly pulled into the lane *while* checking the mirror. The moment she saw the fast-moving car and realized that the car was Matthew's, it was already too late. The impact was quite intense, causing her car to flip over and roll over three times before coming to rest against the tree. He had been travelling at an unreasonably high rate of speed and he simply didn't have time to react to Julianne's entry into his lane. Matthew's car rolled several times and burst into flames.

Part 3

The memorial service was absolutely heart-wrenching. Matthew and Julianne were gone from this world and would be missed tremendously. Families, friends, neighbors and co-workers all trying to understand and cope with the enormity of what had happened. Things like this just aren't supposed to happen. "What a shame," they said. "They will be missed. The neighborhood will never be that same without them." Two urns surrounded by roses; it ripped one's heart out. "They were still so young. They had so much more living to do" everyone agreed, tearfully.

As the memorial service proceeded, a realtor sat patiently in his office, making his notes and putting his numbers together while sketching a rough draft for the newspaper advertisement. Elsewhere in the city, another realtor was gleefully going through the same motions—the early bird catches the worm. Detective O'Malley was patiently awaiting the end of his shift while his friends anticipated his arrival at Mohawk Lake, thirty miles north, where they would spend their weekend casting into lily pads for Bass and drinking beer. At the hospital, Jason waved at the employees as they passed by his office and disappeared into the night and unto the dark and winding, northbound highway.

The Interloper

Yesterday, my daughter and I were chatting at the kitchen table, and as she was telling me her story, she referred to a person as an "interloper." She used the word as casually as I would say "walkers." As in, "I saw two walkers this morning as they walked up the driveway." I think you would agree that if she had said, "I saw two interlopers this morning as they interloped up the driveway," that would be a ridiculous use of superfluous language, and I think that we need to correct this undeserved assault on the English vocabulary. In the case of interloper, we should find the person that conceived the word and hold him or her accountable for their assault.

What exactly is an interloper? There are various interpretations out there for your consideration and if you would take the time to read them all, you would come to realize, as I have, that we really can't be absolutely certain about what an interloper actually is, or what an interloper actually does. It's my current understanding that an interloper is *"A person who becomes involved in a place or situation where they are not wanted or considered not to belong."* I'm in agreement with that beautifully explicit description. Prior to this perfect description, I had thought of an interloper as an intruder or a trespasser or a meddler or a busybody, a snoop, or even an invader. Can't an invader just be an invader without having to interlope as well? It seems to me that if a person has been invaded, it's already too late to play the thesaurus word game. Once the invasion has occurred, all the rest is nothing more than useless debate.

I'm sitting on my porch and a stranger walks up my driveway, now finding me sitting on the porch, and begins to tell me how much happier I would be if I were to switch from cable TV to satellite TV. What's the best way to deal with a situation such as this? First, I must take into consideration that I have not posted a No Interloping sign anywhere on my property. Without a posted sign, I can't consider this person in my driveway as a trespasser just as I wouldn't think of my mail delivery person as a trespasser. This person hasn't invaded my property, she has simply walked up the driveway in a non-threatening manner. In a case like this, the person is simply intruding, but in doing so, she has involved herself in a place or situation where she is not wanted.

"Good morning!" she says cheerfully. "Can you give me a few minutes of your time? I'd like to talk to you about your cable service." I tell her, "We don't have cable—or satellite." Sarcastically she challenged me, telling me, "I can see the cable line hanging from the pole to your house; I don't see a dish anywhere, let me talk to you about your satellite options." She has only been on my porch for thirty seconds and has now effectively identified herself as a meddler and a snoop as well as an intruder. If that's not a great definition of an interloper, I don't know what is. I suppose I could have tried to convince her that we use an antenna, but I knew that she would have seen right through that lie. If I would have been inside the house when she arrived at my door, I simply could have ignored the doorbell and this entire incident would have been over with—I could have ended this story right here, after only five paragraphs. But, no. Of course, not. It's never that simple.

I tell her that we are die-hard cable people, and that we are completely satisfied with cable and with our particular cable provider, and we have no intentions of ever making such a drastic, life-altering, completely overwhelming change to satellite TV. I also tell her that we don't want an unsightly dish on our roof, or anywhere else on the property for that matter. Not persuaded that I've convinced her that the conversation can end, I kept rambling. I tell her that we are in the process of listing our home with a realtor and that she could wait a while and then come back to call on the new owners who perhaps would immediately jump at the opportunity to improve the quality of their lives through the miracle of the satellite dish. I think she realized that I was full of it, but I was hoping that she would at least take note of my hint, pick up her sales material and move on. Still, instead of her telling me, "Well then, thank you for talking with me. I'll just be going now, have a nice day" she just stood in front of me, planning her next angle of attack. It was painfully clear that I was being mercilessly interloped by this charming person with her leather-bound notebook and her tendency to not recognize a person's obvious lack of interest in her agenda.

"Please," I said, "I'm just not interested."

She thought for a moment and it appeared to me that she had recognized a lost skirmish when she saw one, but then she abruptly asked me if she could have some water. I sensed that her plan was to use the ensuing two or three minutes of water-fetching to re-group and come again at me using an entirely different tactic, but I excused myself anyways and went into the house for a bottle of water.

I brought the bottle back to the porch only to find she was no longer there. For a fleeting moment, I had a glimmer of hope that she moved on to the next unassuming house, but when I leaned over the side of the porch to view my side yard, there she was, standing at the edge of the flower bed with a tape-measure in one hand and her notebook in the other hand.

"What are you doing?" I said, "Are you looking for something?"

"No," she said, "You know, you could put the dish right about here," indicating the perfect spot for an ugly satellite dish. "That way you won't have to put it on the roof. I know, you don't want a dish on the roof."

"Look," I said, "I don't want a dish anywhere. Not there in my flower bed, not on the roof, not anywhere! What part of *I don't want a dish* are you not understanding?"

She shrugged that comment off with a phony smile and asked me, "How many TVs do you have?"

I was incredulous as I told her, "It doesn't matter how many TVs we have, because we don't want the dish. We. Don't. Want. The. Dish."

She considered my outburst for a moment, stiffening her stature as she said, "Well, that's rude, don't you think?"

"Yes," I said, "I'm sure you think I'm rude. I am truly sorry, but please, just go now. I don't want to talk about this anymore. Here is your water."

She turned on the big, sad-puppy eyes, then gathered her leather-bound notebook and her purse.

She left the water bottle, unopened, on the ground beside the flower bed – a polite way, I suppose, of expressing her thoughts about where I could put the water bottle. As she passed by me on her way to the driveway she spoke quietly, "I'm just trying to make a living here. Can't you just give me a break?"

These damn interlopers! How did this turn into a guilt trip for ME? I tried to tell her, but she wasn't listening! She didn't even have a drink of her water. Geez, ask a person for water and then leave it laying on the ground. Now, that's rude, right? Very rude, don't you agree?

It was perhaps a month after the unfortunate encounter with the satellite TV representative when my wife and I happened to see her at a Sylvester's. She was sitting at the bar with a friend, scribbling something on a napkin. There was no way to avoid her field of vision. We were seated at our table when I saw the Satellite person entering the restrooms area. She made direct eye contact with me despite my failed attempt to hide behind the conveniently large menu. On the plus side, though, she was smiling rather than scowling.

A few minutes later, she came out of the restroom and walked directly toward our table, approaching the table from behind my wife who obviously had no idea of what was about to happen. My fight or flight instinct was ramping up, preparing for the worst.

"Hey! Mr. Powell, how are you?" she asked me cheerfully.

I replied, "Well, I'm fine. It's good to see you." I introduced her to my wife, Sherri, hastily explaining the situation. I said, "How's the satellite TV business going?"

"Well," She said, "I'm not working there anymore. I'm selling storm windows and doors now."

"Well, that's nice." I said, "How's that working out for you?"

She said, "To be honest, it's much better than what I was doing previously." "Well, good for you." I said. She replied, "Hey, maybe sometime I could come back to your place and take a closer look at your windows? And, your doors? I didn't notice when I was there, but do you have glass block in your basement windows?"

Once an interloper, always an interloper, I suppose.

It's two months now since my conversation with her at Sylvester's, and I haven't heard a word from her. I can't sit on my front porch anymore this year, but that's not a problem because it's cold now — too cold for porch sitting. Even if I should decide that I want to sit out there in the cold air, under the gray and gloomy Lake Erie clouds, I wouldn't risk it. Every time our phone rings, I pretend that I'm either not in the house, or I'm in the house but very, very busy – way too busy to answer the phone.

Damn interlopers.

Gerald Moves On

Gerald is in his mid-fifties now, three decades after it all started. He had always felt that something about his life wasn't right. He couldn't put his finger on the problem, but he knew it was there, always there, just below the surface; something was terribly wrong. For most of his adult life, he was convinced that the problem started sometime in his early childhood. Looking back further, though, and reviewing his childhood in meticulous detail, he concluded that his curious anxiety had most likely started a year or two after high school—around twenty years of age.

He supposed that this simply was the way life is supposed to work and nothing to be overly concerned about. "This is the way life is. Life can't get any better than what it is right now." That was Gerald's favorite thing to say. He thought this statement was very clever and that his priceless words of wisdom would someday fall into the same category as other famous historical quotes such as, "Life is what happens when you're busy making other plans. Or, "Always remember that you are absolutely unique, just like everyone else." Gerald is a dreamer. A badly confused dreamer.

Of all the things that confounded Gerald, what puzzled him most was that nobody would talk to him. Nobody ever struck up a casual conversation with him, or complimented him in any way, or invited him into social events, or acknowledged his existence. When Gerald would attempt to initiate a conversation with someone he was always ignored—unnoticed as though he were invisible. Gerald began to consider the possibility that perhaps he actually was invisible – though not invisible to all. This invisibility to some people but not to others was the primary source of his confusion. On rare occasions, there were people who would happily interact with him, but most people would not even acknowledge his presence. "How rude," he thought! "What kind of people could be this rude?"

Occasionally, Gerald would pay an unexpected visit to his sister's home, only to be ignored. Nobody in his sister's home acknowledged him when he arrived or when he departed. When he commented on random fragments of conversation, nobody would acknowledge his contribution. Visiting his sister is something that he had done many times, always expecting different results, of course. A living example of the definition of insanity.

When Gerald was fifty years old, he decided that he would attend his next high school class reunion.

There were previous reunions that Gerald could have attended but, for some reason, he didn't receive the invitations. Fifty, though, seemed to be an appropriate age for a reunion and it seemed crucially important that he should attend. He saw this opportunity as a last chance, and he supposed that, if he waited until the next reunion, sixty years of age would be too late. He decided that he would go, just for the hell of it—it was now or never. When he arrived, there was nobody at the outer door to greet him. He did, however, notice a table near the entrance to the event room where, presumably, he would find his name tag. Most of the tags had been picked up by attendees and a check of the few remaining tags revealed that no tag had been placed there for Gerald, so he simply walked into the room expecting to be approached by someone—anyone.

As usual, Gerald was completely unnoticed. The room was crowded, though, and people were clustered in small groups, laughing, hugging, some were dancing while others chose to gather near the walls and observe the activity from afar rather than participate. Perhaps nobody noticed his entrance? Gerald approached several people expecting to be acknowledged and welcomed into the festivities. Instead the people looked right through him as though he wasn't there. After half an hour of this nonsense Gerald decided that it was time to go. He knew all along that he shouldn't have wasted his time, but Gerald was an optimistic guy taking an outrageous chance. For nothing.

The following morning, Gerald walked the short distance to the front entrance door where he spent his days roaming the hallways and gardens of his Safe Place. He was greeted by the security person.

"Morning, Gerald," said the security guy. "Good morning Bob, another day in paradise?" Bob smiled knowingly and gave Gerald a tilt of his head and sly wink. Gerald never understood the meaning behind the sly wink, but he appreciated the gesture and he always nodded in agreement even though he didn't know what it was that he was agreeing with.

Everyone in the building was friendly and cheerful, as opposed to his usual experience with people outside of the Safe Place. Everyone passed the time by visiting with friends and reminiscing about the good old days. Sometimes Gerald would catch himself thinking that it would be nice if he could just stay here, forever, in this Safe Place where people are pleasant. Gerald had spent most of his adult life here. There was a peculiar atmosphere of enchantment here, like one would experience when returning to their childhood neighborhood or driving past their old elementary school. Everyone here had no trouble seeing him or talking with him. Why couldn't everyone be as nice as these good people?

One day, Gerald had an overwhelming desire to visit the local mall. He had been to the mall once or twice previously and wasn't especially impressed with the concept of mall-shopping. He was not excited about having to enter a large, enclosed area where he would be required to search for a store while distancing himself further from his home with each step.

While making his way through the mall, Gerald came into the presence of a young woman who introduced herself only as Emma. Gerald had been walking past one of the mall benches when he noticed Emma sitting there, not far from him. She was watching him with great interest which turned to heartfelt concern when she quickly understood his circumstances. Emma knew immediately. Emma was a helper, you see; some might call her a guide.

Emma invited Gerald to sit with her. They talked about many things; Gerald told her all about his problems with people that won't speak to him, and about his frustrating visits to his sister's home, and about the miserable class reunion and everything else that was bothering him. After hearing his stories, she told him that she could help him with his frustrating problem—but only if he had a sincere interest in being helped. "Not all people want to be helped." She said. "They're afraid of what they think might happen to them." Gerald told Emma that he wanted to be helped, and that he wasn't afraid of anything happening to him. What else *could* happen? He told Emma that he was lonely and tired - very tired. To this remark, Emma responded, "We have some planning to do." She asked him to meet her on a walking path two days later, at nightfall.

Gerald found his way to the path that Emma had described two days earlier and, as promised, Emma was there, patiently awaiting his arrival. She had been sitting on a wooden bench under a large tree at the top of a sloped trail that led down to a small lake. She greeted Gerald with a hug and asked him if he was ready for what awaited him. Gerald assured Emma that he was ready and that he was happy and comfortable with his decision. Emma took Gerald's hand in hers and they walked together along the trail in the darkness toward the water's edge.

When they arrived at the lake they sat together on a dock for a few minutes as they listened to the crickets and the distant hooting of an owl. There was a full moon this night and the moonlight reflecting on the lake's surface sparkled with the movement of the water. The dock extended forward for several feet and there was a small rowboat securely tied to a post at the end of the dock. Emma took Gerald's hand, "Gerald, it's time. Be happy." They walked together down the pier's length and Emma assisted Gerald as he stepped into the boat. Emma explained that Gerald would have to row to the other side and that he would eventually see a light on the opposite shore guiding him to his destination.

Once again, Emma took Gerald's hand and told him this, "Gerald, you have done well. Be happy. The best is yet to come." Gerald waved to her as he pushed the boat away from the dock with an oar. When he looked again, Emma was gone.

As Gerald reached the half-way point, he was startled when a large owl landed gently on the point of the bow. At the same time, he saw the light on the shore ahead of him, now perhaps one hundred feet away. A minute later, when he reached the dock, the owl took flight, disappearing into the night sky. As the bow touched the side of the dock, Gerald noticed a person coming forward out of the shadows. Gerald extended his arm to grasp the hand of his father who helped him onto the dock. For some reason, Gerald was neither scared nor suspicious. "I've been expecting you, son. What took you so long?" They walked together along a trail that opened to a magnificent sunrise, swirls of golden orange and pink kissing the clouds, with a mountain peak in the distance. Gerald was speechless. He'd never seen such amazing beauty.

As they walked toward the amazing sunrise, they eventually came to a beautiful garden which seemed to go on forever. In front of Gerald there was a vast landscape showing miles upon miles of deep green, rolling hills all covered in wildflowers. They entered the garden to the left and followed the trail eventually emerging to another enormous, garden where he saw many beautiful peacocks walking among people that were smiling and chatting as they strolled through the most beautiful flowers he had ever seen. At the far edge of the garden he saw an incredible palace that rolled on toward the horizon. In front of this palace there was a large patio where people were sitting and enjoying the views and the beautiful music that filled the air in every part of this glorious place. Many people came to Gerald, introducing themselves and engaging him in conversation. Gerald was giddy with happiness.

Years passed. One morning as Gerald was sitting on a bench in a lovely courtyard, where he went every morning to watch the incredible sunrise, he heard a familiar voice behind him. He felt the weight of a person sliding onto his bench shortly followed by the feel of something soft against his skin. He turned to look and found a woman there, smiling at him.

Such an incredibly beautiful smile—so beautiful, in fact, it hurt his heart and moved him to tears. "Gerald, how are you?" she asked. Gerald recognized Emma immediately, even though so many years had passed since their last time together at the water's edge. "What took you so long?" he asked her.

"I had my work to finish," Emma whispered.

Mr. Murphy's Garden

I think it's safe to say that Mr. Murphy sits in his garage a lot. More than most people would, I think. As far as I know, Mr. Murphy doesn't sit in the garage at night, only in the daytime, although last summer I did see him in there one night around 9:30 p.m. – but only that one time. I don't look for him in the winter simply because I have no reason to use Overland Avenue outside of the summer season. Come winter, Overland Avenue, which Mr. Murphy's garage faces, is cold and icy and completely unlit – not ideal driving conditions in Ohio. Mr. Murphy's house is on the same street that I use when driving to the Sanctuary golf course, which luckily for me, is a mere five-minute drive from my house, and golf in Ohio is generally a Summer-only sport. For the first three months after my initial sighting of him, Mr. Murphy didn't react when he noticed my car, and then one day he waved as I passed his house, and I returned the gesture.

In the summer, weather permitting, I walk on Sunday mornings. Usually around 9:00 a.m., I will set out on my journey and return to my house about an hour later. My walking route takes me past Mr. Murphy's house and I see him in his garage every

Sunday, sitting in his cushioned patio chair, reading his morning paper and enjoying his coffee. On rare occasions, I have seen him roaming in his front yard, checking his bird feeders while stretching his legs. Last Sunday morning, while walking past his house, he waved at me and motioned to me that I should join him in his garage. He placed a second chair next to his own chair, both on a large circular rug. His car was parked on the opposite side of this two-car attached garage.

As I walked down his driveway toward the garage, he stood to greet me, extending his hand in a gesture of welcome. "I'm Jack Murphy, welcome to my world. Have a seat and take a load off." I shook his hand, introducing myself and explaining that I didn't want to impose on his morning *alone* time. "Don't be ridiculous," He said, "You're not imposing, and *all* of my time is alone time. Would you like some coffee?" I replied that I had to finish my walk and go home because two birds had been trapped in our rain gutter. I explained that I had to remove two sections of our gutter guards so the birds could be freed to fly away. "Really?!" He said. "That's quite unusual. How did they become trapped?" I told him that I had no idea how it could have happened. Our gutters are covered with heavy screen, all of which is firmly attached along the inside and outside edges and at each end. There was no way for birds to get into the gutters and be trapped. "It's a mystery!" I said. "I really have no idea."

I proceeded to give Mr. Murphy the narrative of my morning thus far. "When I had awakened on that Sunday morning, I stayed in bed debating the possibility of getting another hour of sleep when I heard the scratching on metal. At first, it sounded like something had somehow gotten inside of the overhang between the outer wall of the house and the edge of the roof, perhaps a squirrel. I put a ladder up and inspected the entire roof overhang finding nothing out of the ordinary – no points of entry. Then I climbed onto the roof and walked along the edge of the roof, eventually finding two small birds huddled together, absolutely terrified, trying desperately to blend in with the bottom of the aluminum gutter. Their screeching mother was in a tree about fifty feet from where the baby birds were. I started to remove a section of the gutter guard that was directly above the two birds, but this panicked the birds even more. I moved several feet along the roof edge, away from the birds, toward the back of the house, where I removed two sections of the gutter guard so the birds could escape. Not wanting to panic them any further, I climbed down and went on with my morning, planning to check later on the status of the birds."

I told Mr. Murphy that I changed clothes and left the house for my walk, and that now I needed to go home to check on the birds. "Well, that's the craziest thing I've ever heard." He said. "Will you let me know how everything turned out? I'll be thinking about this all day." I said I was sure that eventually the birds would escape, unharmed hopefully, and that I would stop by and give him an update.

The birds did escape. When I got home, I climbed the ladder and walked the roofline as before and found no birds in the gutter. I replaced the gutter guard at the two places I had uncovered and then began my descent on the ladder. When I reached what I thought was the last rung, I stepped off the ladder expecting to find solid ground under my feet but discovered that I had two more rungs to go before finding solid ground. Bottom line — I twisted my right knee and did something to my right hip as well. I'm okay, but dammit. Anyway, now I had a good excuse to justify any bad golf swings that may or may not occur in the coming weeks.

So, a few days later I fortified myself with a generous dose of Extra Strength Tylenol and decided that I would take a short walk and maybe go past Mr. Murphy's garage again. In due course, I drew near to Murphy's driveway and observed that he was where I'd always seen him – in the chair, in the shade, in the garage. He motioned for me to join him. After completing the obligatory handshake, we sat down, and he asked me about the birds. I assured him that the birds had flown away to safety and everything was back to normal. I also told him about my ladder mishap and he suggested that if the truth were known, every man, at some point in his life, has done what he referred to as the "ladder long-step" and we both laughed.

He asked me if I wanted coffee, and while I did, I didn't want to bother him. "No thanks," I said, "I'm coffee overdosed as we speak." He wasn't hearing any of that. "I'm not going to poison you, if that's what you're thinking." I acquiesced, saying, "Sure, why not, but only if you don't have to brew another pot. Light on the poison, please." He brought me a full steaming mug along with some individual serving sugar packets that we see in restaurants, and a small carton of coffee creamer.

After reclaiming his chair, he asked me about myself and I told him that I was retired, still happily married, and about my daughter and her husband losing their home in northern California as a result of a wildfire and deciding to resettle on some acreage south of Canton. He informed me that he is a widower, and that his only child, a daughter, his son-in-law and granddaughter were living in Amsterdam.

He complained about the fact that they never call or come home for a visit, spinning his complaint to the usual "I know they're very busy" excuse. He explained that several years ago, his son-in-law accepted an executive-level engineering position there – a job that was impossible to for him pass up.

He told me he hadn't been alone that whole time, as he used to have a dog, Bucky, who had passed away about five years ago. He had buried Bucky in the garden. He pointed out that Bucky was resting in what actually used to be the garden. Mr. Murphy stopped working the garden several years ago due to some minor leg problems. It became overgrown so it was now mowed along with the rest of the grass by a guy who rode a "stand-up" mower; way too much mower than needed for his relatively small lot. Probably even too much mower for a football field, but what do I know. I *push* my mower.

Mr. Murphy decided that he wanted to show me the spot where old Bucky was resting (he calls it resting, I call it buried) in the backyard, the same place that Bucky loved and faithfully defended against crazy chipmunks and angry birds. I could see a slight hump in the ground, indicating that Mr. Murphy might have been a bit over-enthusiastic with the fill dirt. I was reminded of visiting my father's grave when I was a kid. I could see the hump and when walking over it, there was a noticeable deviation in height from the surrounding ground. However, a year later as the ground settled, there was no longer a hump at his gravesite. Mr. Murphy told me that Bucky had passed away five years ago. The hump surely should have leveled-out by now, but there it was, stubbornly defying gravity.

Mr. Murphy (let's just call him Jack from here on, shall we?) told me that he grew tomatoes in his garden prior to experiencing his health problems. He told me that I was welcome to use his garden area should I ever decide to become a gardener. He told me that he would be able to maintain the plantings but not able to do the actual tilling, shoveling, planting and the other unpleasant stuff. As much as I appreciated his offer, I knew deep down that he was hustling me — but in a nice way. He proposed that I could do the heavy work and he would busy himself caring for the plants – spraying, pruning, watering, fertilizing, all the easy stuff. Ultimately, I agreed to help him in his garden because I needed the exercise and Jack needed something to do with his time.

I told Jack that I wouldn't be able to do the tilling, but I was willing to take on the rest of the planting process. He said that he "had a guy" that would do the tilling. I would bet that "the guy" is the very same guy that uses the stand-up mower, and this told me to be expecting a bulldozer in the garden.

A week later, and then another week later, the garden had not been tilled. A third week later, and still no tilling had been done. When I asked Jack about the setback, he said that maybe we should just forget the whole thing. After all it would soon be getting close to late-summer and probably too late to plant anything. Maybe next year, though.

"Want some coffee?" he asked. I abstained. Jack said, "You know, in early summer, before the humidity sets in, all is pleasant and comfortable, the air is clear, and everything is bright and fresh as far as weather is concerned. But now it's getting to be too hot and the humidity has set in and it's just, I don't know, just awful." He paused, before adding, "actually, I don't like tomatoes that much. I must have been thinking that you were the one who liked tomatoes." I told Jack it was okay that he had changed his mind about the gardening project, and I confessed that I wasn't excited about the gardening project either.

The days passed. Later in the summer, just before Labor Day, I stopped at Jack's house. I didn't see him in the garage as usual, so I went around the house to the back yard where I saw Jack sitting in one of those tubular aluminum, vinyl-strapped lawn chairs. He was sitting in the area that had once been an abandoned garden but was now the resting place for Bucky. He was sitting near where the hump had been. Apparently, Jack had raked the debris away and (finally) leveled out the hump. Jack had then planted some wildflowers, enough to cover the entire area where the hump had been, then he had mulched everything. The next thing I noticed was the small gravestone that had not previously been there. The stone was set at what I presumed to be the head of the plot. I read the newly-carved lettering: "Bucky, my friend, I miss you 2004 – 2015."

Jack said "What do you think about the stone? Is it too much?" I said, "It's a beautiful stone, and the flowers make this a perfect place and hopefully they will spread all through the area." Eventually, I told him that I try not to think about losing my four-pawed friend, Spencer, even though I know it's coming. Soon. I told him, "He's twelve now, you know." "Yea, I know," he said. "It's hard." Then he declared, "I really don't want a garden here. I like it just the way it is. What do you think?" I said, "Jack, It's your garden. Bucky probably didn't like tomatoes, anyway."

Mr. Murphy smiled.

* * *

"Dogs come into our lives to teach us about love, they depart to teach us about loss. A new dog never replaces an old dog, it merely expands the heart. If you have loved many dogs your heart is very big."

~ Erica Jong

Jack Calloway

Jack was in one of his unpleasant moods again today. Some days his temperament is terrible; so awful in fact, I sometimes feel compelled to hide from him; while other days he appears to be as cheerful as anyone could ever hope to be. I probably should have dealt with his mood swings a long time ago, but I had failed to do so and that's on me; I know that and, unfortunately, the employees know that as well. Even Abigail, his late wife, may she rest in peace, knew this. He performs his job duties satisfactorily; he knows what to do and exactly how to do whatever has to be done, so I'm not complaining about his job performance. My only problem with him is with his unpredictable moods — he's up, he's down, he's somewhere in between, I never know what to expect. Furthermore, he has this very annoying habit of sitting at his desk while flossing his teeth with a rubber band that he keeps in the lap drawer of his workstation along with paperclips and pencils. Who knows how many times that rubber band has been reused?

After months of intense deliberation, I have at last decided that I'm going to sell this business in one more year. I can't do this anymore. I'm tired and burned out and sometimes I think I'm probably as ill-tempered as Jack. I always try to control my temperament as any reasonable person would — the same as the employees would do and the same as you, my reader, would do. Simply said, "we accept responsibility for our behavior."

I'm not a licensed therapist, I'm a business owner. It wasn't my responsibility nor calling in life to figure out Jack. If there had been a time when I wanted to listen to his problems, I'd have become a licensed psychiatrist charging outrageous fees and spending my weekends in a big house on a big beautiful lake with an incredible boat.

Having said all of this, and in all due fairness to Jack, I must tell you that when Jack is in one of his better moods, not only is he a tolerable fellow, he is actually quite pleasant. On rare occasions when I had been to lunch with Jack — on one of his "good mood" days — I can truthfully say that I even enjoyed his company. On other rare occasions when he insisted on picking up the check, I noticed that he was a very generous tipper and he was always authentically polite to the servers; in fact, sometimes he would include a server in our private conversations as though we were all close friends. Jack could be a delightful person.

Last Wednesday afternoon, Jack called me on my office phone, even though his office is only two doors down from my office. He asked me if perhaps I would have an interest in having a burger with him at the pub, three blocks up the street from the office — the very same pub where we have our occasional lunches. I told Jack that I could meet him there after work, but I wouldn't be able to stay very long because I have other things to do. I have a life and a happy home. The truth is, I can't keep up with Jack and his moods anymore. I stopped trying years ago. It has degenerated to this: He works, I give him a paycheck, and that's the end of story.

The pub was nearly packed to capacity, given it was after 5; it was not the usual lunch bunch but, rather, a more boisterous and youthful group of people who had apparently taken control. This was the Happy Hour mob, an altogether diverse variety of pub customer. We ordered our food and discussed mundane things, world events, politics and so forth, and then he told me about his day. He explained that he had set his bedside clock for a 6:30 a.m. wake-up, but this morning he found himself fully conscious and hyper-alert long before the time of his intended awakening. He had been trying to sleep since he had been frightened to wakefulness, at 4:50. He was tired — exhausted, really, but his mind refused to slow down, not even for just one more hour of sleep. He told me that he had "the dream" again.

When I asked Jack what he meant by "the dream," he told me that he frequently dreams of an intruder entering his house and hiding, watching him sleep, seemingly waiting for him to awaken. When he does wake up, he is nearly paralyzed with fear. I asked Jack if the intruder ever threatens him in any way. "No," he said. "Whatever it is, it never speaks a word. I've never seen the thing, but I always know when it's there. I can feel its presence." He told me that it's a frightening experience because he can't see his visitor and therefor doesn't know exactly where the thing is. Is it beside him? Is it behind him? Above him? No way to know.

I told him a memory I had from when I was a kid. I was fishing off a rock bank at a local reservoir, sitting on a rock when something started nibbling on my bait, causing the bobber to dance on the water's surface. I moved down from the rock so I could move a little closer to the water's edge when, suddenly, an overpowering feeling of dread came over me. Every part of me was screaming that I should freeze and then slowly shuffle backward — which I did, very slowly. When I looked downward and perhaps three or four feet from where I had been walking, I saw a coiled Copperhead snake, poised to strike. The snake and I locked into direct eye contact and neither of us moved a muscle. Its eyes were locked onto my eyes. Even to this day, I think of that sense of dread. I didn't see the snake at first because it blended in with the rocks. I will never forget those unnerving eyes. "Is that the kind of dread you're talking about? You can feel it throughout your body?" I asked Jack. He confirmed that I was absolutely correct in my description of his reaction to "the dream."

Jack also told me that he has been having this nightmare more frequently than usual and because of these annoying "additional" interruptions of his sleep, he has been more irritable and bad tempered than usual.

It was obvious to me that he wasn't coping with his wife's death and I wish there was something I could do for him, but I'm not a professional. What can I do for him?

I have a friend whose name is Ashley and this person is somewhat unconventional in the sense that she is deeply involved in the art and science of life after death. Ashley is convinced that occasionally spirits of the departed can be trapped here, in this dimension, somewhere between physical death and life beyond death. On the other side of this coin, I am convinced there are no spirits trapped anywhere, for any reason. Ashley respects my opinion and in appreciation of that, I respect her point of view as well. Over the years, she and I have had many discussions on this subject, all of which have ultimately gone off the rails and into the cornfield.

Ashley told me about a woman, Anne Wallace, living in the downtown Brownstone neighborhood known as Little Brooklyn, a one-mile stretch of bricked streets where you will find lovely brownstone Towne Houses similar to what we would see while enjoying an afternoon stroll through a typical Brooklyn, New York neighborhood. There are stately trees and well-kept front gardens, and it is entirely pleasant there. If you were to go to Little Brooklyn seeking amusement, though, you might be disappointed unless you are expecting to find Anne Wallace, in which case you might strike gold. Anne Wallace is a one-in-a-million, very special person, so says Ashley.

Ashley explained that when you arrive at Mrs. Wallace's address, you will have a climb of perhaps twelve steps to her the doorway, where you will ring the doorbell in order to request an audience with Anne, a widow of perhaps sixty years of age. Once identified, you will be buzzed into the hallway, which you will follow to her apartment door on the right. Anne waits for her visitors while standing behind her partially opened door, always secured by two door chains. Ashley further explained that Mrs. Wallace doesn't make any special claims about who she is or what she does. In fact, she told Ashley that with practice and commitment, anyone can do what she does, but I don't believe that.

I've tried doing whatever it is that Anne does many times, always without success. I even sought the knowledge of Google:

Psychic: "A psychic is a person who claims to have a supernatural ability to perceive events in the future or beyond normal sensory contact."

I am mostly interested in the "beyond normal sensory contact" aspect of the definition. So, with these thoughts in mind, I think it's safe to say that Anne is a Psychic Medium—one who communicates with deceased people. And so, this is how I've decided to define Anne Wallace.

I can't help Jack, but I was wondering if Anne Wallace could. So, this morning I called Jack on his office phone, even though my office is only two doors down from his. I asked him to come in for a chat when he had some time and he arrived at my doorway within 15 seconds after I hung up. I told Jack that I might have found a person, who he might want to meet with for a chat regarding his frequent night-time dream visitor. Of course, Jack wanted to know everything about this person, and I explained that she is supposedly able to make contact with spirits that have become trapped between death and life beyond death. I told him everything I knew about Anne Wallace — Little Brooklyn, the townhouse and everything else that I could recall from my conversations with Ashley. He seemed genuinely interested and not at all suspicious. He agreed to a meeting.

When Jack approached Anne's partially opened door, she greeted him as if they were old friends; two friends perhaps reestablishing an old companionship. She stood aside as Jack passed through the doorway, "Welcome, come in. We'll be going to my office, straight ahead and to your left." They walked through her well-appointed apartment to a smallish room where Jack saw walls of shelving, all of which covered with books of all varieties. Some of these books were expensive, leather-bound editions, some were hardback and many more were paperback. There was no table between Jack and Anne as one would expect to see at a "Psychic" reading. Instead, they sat in comfortable wingback chairs facing across from each other and separated by a low, round coffee table. In the center of this table there was a large candle resting on a tiled tray, as well as a flower floating in a clear glass bowl.

As Jack settled into a chair, Anne asked, "Shall I spook it up a little? Do you like candles?" Jack replied, "Whatever you usually do is fine with me." She lit the candle and soon the burning wax filled the room with a delightful fragrance of fruit—freshly squeezed oranges, actually.

"Tell me about yourself." Anne said. Jack responded, "Really, there isn't much to tell about myself, other than I am having problems sleeping." Jack explained that he was having nightmares, then awakening and feeling the presence of someone or something in his bedroom. Anne replied, "We'll just sit here and have a very nice talk. Nothing is off-limits here. Everything we discuss in this room, stays in this room."

Jack said, "I occasionally reach for my phone just before it rings. I don't know how or why this is happening." Anne looked at him as if she were expecting something more exciting for them to talk about. Jack said, "I know it's silly and I'm sorry to disappoint you. Really, there's more than this — a lot more." Anne told Jack this phone issue was a perfect place to start, and they would continue down this path until they found another trail to follow. Jack said, "I don't know how much more could be said about the phone. I threw the phone thing out there in an effort to start the proverbial ball rolling." Jack explained further, "For no particular reason, I feel compelled to pick up my phone and when I reach for the phone, it rings. When this happens, there are never any "pre-ring" phone thoughts in my mind. I suddenly know that I should grab my phone." Anne then said, "Is this a transient thing, or do these phone incidents occur regularly over a long period of time, months perhaps?" Jack explained that the phone incidents were, unfortunately, temporary, lasting for no more than six months at most. Having heard this bit of crucial information, Anne asked Jack to explain what happens after answering his phone and saying Hello? "Nothing of interest happens," Jack said, "I heard no voices or breathing or any other background noise. Only dead air." As an afterthought, he further explained that on three occasions, he heard something, static possibly, that sounded like ocean waves, but he couldn't be sure about that. "Then," Jack said, "The visions began around the same time that the phone calls stopped."

"Stop right there!" Anne said, moving her chair closer to the table. She leaned in a little closer and asked, "What visions? Tell me about these visions." He explained that his visions were "internal," in other words, seen behind his closed eyelids. Anne asked, "What, exactly. have you been seeing behind your closed eyes?" Jack responded, "Beautiful scenery.

Incredibly beautiful scenery." Anne asked if there was something specific to see, such as mountains, deserts, or perhaps cities. Jack explained that there was nothing but wilderness; extremely beautiful, virgin wilderness, as far as his eyes could see. He further explained that he was seeing all of this from above. "I was floating above the ground at different heights of my own choosing. At first, I was up so high I could see continents and oceans. Nothing looked familiar, though. There was no north and south America, or Africa, or India, or China. It was not our planet that I was observing. I could float lower as well; close to the treetops but for some reason I was not able, or not permitted, to lower myself all the way to the ground."

He continued, "I saw lakes, rivers, streams. It was amazing. I could drift along above a stream and follow it to a lake. The sky was a deep blue and completely cloudless." Jack took a deep breath and continued, "The sunlight was clear and crisp, like seeing the beauty of it all in high definition. No structures or highways and no herds of animals were seen. I asked to see a bird and immediately a very large bird appeared in the lower right corner of my field of vision and flew toward the upper left corner. It seemed to be flying in slow motion. It was hard to tell if it was actually moving in slow motion because it was so large. Or, perhaps I wanted to see it in that motion because it pleased me."

Jack continued, "I had an awareness that some-one or some-thing was there with me, showing these things to me. I mentally asked this someone, "Where do you live?" I was thinking that if this entity would show its home to me, I might see villages or maybe even entire cities, but this was not to be the case. Immediately after asking this question, I found myself in another place where there was no sunshine. It was night but when I looked at the sky, I saw beautiful streaks of light, all colors and shapes, shooting and rolling and flashing through the dark, night sky in multiple directions. The light was diffused, as if I was watching the lights through a fine mist. In this place, I was able to stand on the ground, walk on a dirt path, and I sat on a flat outcrop of rock while mentally chatting with my invisible guide. The diffused light was bright enough that I could see shadows moving around me and I felt the presence of other persons as well. There was no noise in this place; only perfect and total silence."

Anne was sitting on the edge of her chair, looking at Jack through curious eyes, possibly surprised eyes or suspicious eyes? Hearing himself describe his visions out loud, Jack suddenly felt a bit foolish and quite uncomfortable. He considered making a quick exit when Anne said, "Jack, you've told me that when you were experiencing the silent world where you saw the amazing lights, you were accompanied by a someone, an entity, an invisible guide, and a something. I'm assuming you were referring to one individual and not all of the above." Jack replied that he was referring to an invisible guide who showed up apparently from nowhere and, he believed, was there to protect and perhaps enlighten him. Jack said, "I felt safe knowing that someone was watching over me. I felt loved" Anne replied, "So, you accept that someone was there with you, and they exchanged not voice, but thought transference with you? You accept that the invisible guide meant you no harm?" Jack replied that he accepted all her suggestions as accurate. Anne continued, "You also told me that while you were still in the beautiful place where you were looking down at the forest and the rivers, you asked to see an animal of some kind, and then a large bird appeared in your field of vision." Jack replied that he did, in fact, mention the bird experience.

"JACK!" She shouted, surprising herself, "I've just seen something absolutely beautiful! It hit me like a hammer!" She continued, "I saw a beautiful beach, and I saw, in the distance, a young woman running along the ocean's edge where damp sand meets foamy water. She was running in "real" motion and moving, "flapping" if you will, her arms up and down in "slow" motion — like a very large bird. She was laughing uncontrollably as she aimlessly floated gracefully through the imaginary sky along the water's edge — without a doubt, her very best imitation of a sea gull swooping in for a landing. She's running toward a handsome young man who awaits her landing. He is also laughing at the sight of this girl who is imagining herself as a large bird. I suggest the young man is you and the beautiful young woman is Abigail. The two of you are at the beach. Jack, this is what I have seen, but there's more." Jack informed Anne that she was correct. Jack and Abigail spent their honeymoon at Fort Myers, Florida. He remembered that day, thirty-five years ago, as though it was only last week. They were both euphoric. It was the happiest day of their lives. Jack asked, "You said that you saw something else on the beach; what else did you see there?"

Anne said, "I saw you and Abigail, walking hand-in hand into the water. Abigail was kicking the water and playfully jumping up and down. When the two of you reached chest-high water you both stopped and looked ahead toward the horizon. Then you both jumped upward and splashed down, under the surface. A second later you both popped up. Abigail was still holding her nose; she hated having water in her nose. Then I saw the two of you face each other and go under the surface, like before. A few seconds later, you came up for air. Abigail wasn't with you. You appeared to be a bit heaver with graying hair, and certainly not euphoric. You faced the horizon and my vision stopped there as rapidly as it started. I'm sorry, I can't tell you more. That's all I was able to see.

Jack's eyes were welling, but he was composed when he asked, "Anne, what does all of this mean?" Softly, Anne replied, "I won't promise you that any of what I am going to suggest is fact. It simply is what it is, I can't make it any clearer than that. I can tell you my thoughts, but you have to decide for yourself what it means to you." "Yes, of course! I understand completely." Jack said, "Please tell me!" Anne began, "Jack, the simplest way to put this is to say that you and Abigail made a life together, but Abigail wasn't able go the distance with you. Her body couldn't stay here any longer and she had to leave you alone. She didn't have a choice — you see that, right? Perhaps my visualization of Abigail's failure to re-surface from the water could mean she can't come back into this world, but she can be with you this way — the way things are now." Anne told Jack he shouldn't be terrified of his dreams and that if someone wanted to harm him, they most certainly would have done so by now.

Anne's information overloaded Jack's circuitry. He reclaimed his chair and gazed at the scented candle for a minute or two while he considered everything Anne had said. He was hoping that Anne was correct in her assumptions. He had been persuaded to accept that his nocturnal visitor was not someone or something seeking to harm him. Instead, he believed that Abigail's dead-air phone calls and nocturnal visits were her way of metaphorically coming up from below the surface. This, he supposed, was her way of telling him that she indeed was still alive. Anne finished with, "Jack, she's simply in another room right now, and you don't have the key." Jack was delighted.

Jack hasn't snapped at me, or anyone else for that matter, in six months. I have a very good feeling about Jack's future, and I think that Jack feels the same way. He and I don't go to lunch anymore. Every day, weather permitting, Jack spends his lunch hour in a nearby park, on a bench that overlooks a small lagoon and sometimes he wanders across the small, wooden bridge and sits contented on a flat rock, near the water's edge. Life is good now. I have been reconsidering the sale of my business. Maybe I should work for a few more years. What the hell. I want that damn boat.

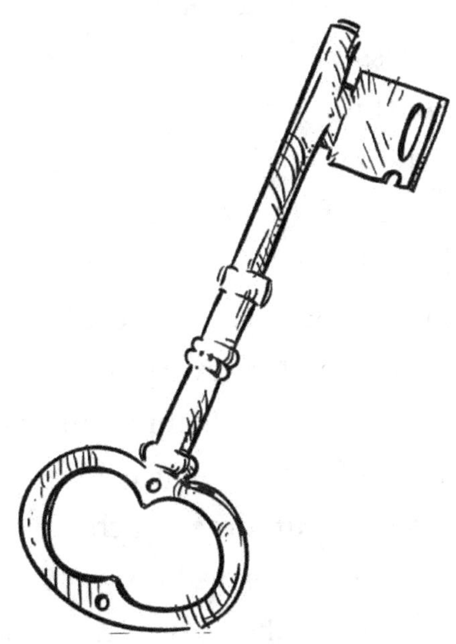

Miserable Charles

Charles is a miserable failure. I know that sounds a bit harsh here in the very first sentence, on the very first page of this story, but I'm telling you the truth as I understand it at this point in time. He didn't realize that he was a failure, nor that he was miserable, until he had become too old to rectify his circumstances. He was hopelessly lost and couldn't find his way back to the past nor forward into the future. Charles had always thought of himself as a cheerful and somewhat successful person. It was within this revised view of his world that he was suddenly and unexpectedly struck by an extraordinary thought. Charles had decided that everything he had done in the pursuit of success and contentment was a complete waste of time. A waste of time and a waste of his life – the only lifetime which would ever be granted to him, as far as we know. "We get only one ride on the pony," as they say. The music plays, the big wheel turns, and when it stops, you slide out of the saddle and fade into oblivion. Poof!

For the first two weeks under the influence of this new self-hating mindset, he was convinced that he was simply going through a rough patch and that eventually the blue skies would return, and all would be as it should. Another week later he was still feeling the effects of his self-imposed failure. In fact, things seemed to be taking a turn for the worse. In response to this setback, he decided that he would pay a visit to his favorite tavern on Portage street where he would sit quietly, enjoy a beer, think about his problem and perhaps find a way out of this troublesome situation. Maybe two beers. He was thinking that it would be nice to see some of his old friends there and they would drink some beer, have some laughs, and he would go home with a more positive outlook on life in general, and on his life in particular.

As usual, the parking lot was very near full, but he was able to find a spot at the extreme south end of the lot – on the grass. He locked his car and made his way to the bar which appeared to be seated to full capacity, but as luck would have it, there was one barstool available and this is where he chose to sit – not that he actually had a choice. After three minutes on this stool he understood why the seat was vacant – it was located directly under a ceiling-mounted air conditioning duct. It wasn't that bad, though. Sure, the air was frigid, but he thought of himself as a tough old guy and he supposed that he could handle the cool air on the top of his head and the back of his neck and shoulders without whining like a baby.

The bartender was extremely busy and after Charles had waited for what he considered to be an unreasonably long period of time, she finally caught a glimpse of him, sitting there patiently, under the ceiling duct. "What can I getcha, Hon?" He said that he would like a Heineken, then he asked her if there was a way to shut off the overhead air duct. She said, "I'll check, Hon." He watched her pull his frosty bottle from the cooler and bring it to him, along with a hastily grabbed glass and the obligatory paper coaster. She didn't check with anyone about the duct and this annoyed him, but it was a very busy evening and he could easily see that she was extremely busy. Much too busy to care about closing the air duct as a favor for a grumpy old guy.

He decided that he wouldn't make a scene and try to make the best of it, but then a feeling of dread came over him. He realized this whole thing was a very bad idea. None of his old buddies would have been there because most of them were dead, and the ones who weren't dead had relocated to Florida and South Carolina. He knew that he should simply finish his Heineken, or not, and move on. He didn't leave a tip.

As he was pulling out of the parking lot, he was suddenly struck by an almost uncontrollable urge for a mocha chip ice cream treat, but at the same time he was disillusioned because he knew from past experience that the local ice cream proprietor was either unable or unwilling to produce a proper Mocha Chip treat. Albert Einstein is credited with saying, "The definition of insanity is doing the same thing over and over again but expecting different results." Charles decided that he would, once again, try for that ever-elusive "proper" mocha chip. He promised himself this would be the very last time. The very last time.

He entered the ice cream parlor, went directly to the counter and ordered his usual small dish of mocha chip. He found a table close to the back of the parlor and next to a window. After a few minutes, a server delivered his small dish of Mocha Chip. He immediately looked at the ice cream, noting the color – pure white (again) with a light sprinkling of chocolate chips. He was immediately disappointed, but he optimistically and hopefully sampled the ice cream, wishing for a "different result." As expected, it was the usual plain old vanilla with chocolate chips. He gathered the dish, patted his pockets to assure himself that his car keys were still there, and walked to the service counter. The employee who served him stepped helpfully toward him to ask if everything was okay, but he stopped her in her tracks, demanding that he speak with the manager.

A minute or two later, a man appeared in the window of the doorway that separated the customer area from the kitchen. Charles could see the man talking to the employee who had served him the mocha-less ice cream. When the man approached, Charles asked him if he was the manager and was then informed that the man was the owner of this establishment. He asked, "What can I do for you?" Charles replied that over the last three years he had ordered perhaps twenty Mocha Chip ice creams from this establishment, all of which contained no mocha. He explained that he was receiving only vanilla ice cream and (very few) chocolate chips, but no mocha. The owner thought for a moment and then replied that they don't serve "caffeine products." Charles said, "If you don't serve caffeine products, why does your menu offer a 'Mocha' flavored ice cream?" The owner asked Charles if he would prefer a refund or a store credit. Charles turned away from the counter and walked out of the establishment, silently vowing never to return. He didn't leave a tip.

Charles was not in the mood to go home, so he decided that he would take a short ride during which he would turn off the air conditioner and enjoy the fresh air rolling into his car through the open front windows. He headed east beyond the city limits and turned north on Middlebranch Avenue. As he was passing through the center of this tiny, pin-point dot on the map he noticed the middle-school which reminded him of his childhood and the ball games he played during recess. He recalled one particular incident when the self-appointed team captain – usually the largest and toughest kid on the playground – sent Charles out to center field to relieve a player, Butch Cooper, who appeared to be dropping the ball, both literally and figuratively; mostly literally.

Charles recalled trotting toward center field, glove in hand, noticing that Butch was watching his approach with curiosity and, Charles thought, a bit of agitation as well. Upon his arrival at his designated playing position, he informed Butch that he had been sent there, by the captain, to relieve him. Butch said nothing in response to Charles' message from the captain. Instead, Butch simply stared at Charles as though he was attempting to hypnotize him, or perhaps make him disappear. Charles didn't know what else to say; he was only the messenger. It wasn't like he had made the decision to remove Butch from center field. Butch considered Charles' message from the team captain for a moment and then punched Charles in the stomach. After recovering his ability to inhale, Charles surmised that Butch's gut punch was most likely what the team captain had anticipated would happen if the captain himself had gone to center field to deliver his own message to Butch. Lesson learned. This is why the Sergeant always sends the Corporal to deliver bad news to the squad.

As Charles made his way back into the North Canton area, he decided that he should go home and discus his negative mindset with his wife, who always seemed to have the right answers. "How was your evening out," she asked. Charles told her about the air conditioning duct, and the mocha-less ice cream, and about his recollection of the 8th grade stomach punch on the ball field while she sat patiently listening to his story.

After digesting his description of the evening, his wife opened the discussion with a question regarding the ice cream. "Really?" She said. "You're still bitching about the mocha chip thing?" She then suggested that he had two choices regarding the matter of Mocha Chip ice cream. "First," she said, "Just stop going there. Go somewhere else. Drive down to Canton and get your Mocha Chip at that place on Fulton Road. Or, give up Mocha Chip. Let it go; it was a good ride but it's over now. You like the chocolate/peanut butter, don't you?" she asked. Charles responded that, yes, he did have a serious weakness for chocolate/peanut butter ice cream.

Further she said, "I'm still working three days a week while you are obsessing over Mocha Chip, of all things. I wish that was all I had to worry about. You see that, right? It's ice cream?" she continued to lecture him. Yes, Charles was aware of that. It was a good ride but it's over. And he shouldn't be complaining about petty issues. Luckily for Charles, his wife failed to open the can of worms regarding his complaining every morning about the "damn paper guy" dropping the paper on the sidewalk in front of the house, (intentionally, Charles was sure of) as opposed to placing it where a morning newspaper belongs – on the front porch, at the door.

His wife, however, was not done with her lecture. She next reminded him that thirty years ago, at Long Beach Island, New Jersey, when challenged by an annoying air conditioning duct, he stubbornly refused to leave. He insisted that all would be well once they had become "acclimated" to the frigid air. They simply should have gone somewhere else – but no. They stayed and he was miserable for the entire week with a sore throat. Regarding his recent local tavern visit, she asked him, "why would you just sit there, at the bar, with Arctic air freezing your flesh when – and here's an ingenious idea – you simply could have gone somewhere else?" she asked him. He did leave the bar eventually and go to the ice cream parlor, but only dug his hole deeper.

Regarding the ball field episode (also way back in the last century), his wife asked Charles if he had said or done something to irritate Butch Cooper, to which Charles replied that he had done no such thing. He told her that he had barely known Butch Cooper and always tried avoid him. Charles explained that the kids called Butch, "Bad-Ass Butch Cooper." His wife suggested that perhaps Butch really wasn't a bad-ass tough guy after all, and that possibly he was, at some point in time, a victim of tough guy aggression, and that perhaps Butch developed his own way of coping with tough guy aggression – real or imagined. His wife said, "Honey, are you sure you didn't say something to him, something rude or embarrassing or threatening?" "No," Charles said. "I mean, I wasn't aggressive about it, but I was just so pumped up with the idea that I had been selected to replace Bad Ass-Butch Cooper. Well," Charles conceded, "maybe I had a slightly, very tiny, condescending attitude?" His wife said, "Well, did you? Did you have an attitude? Everyone has feelings, you know," she chided him, gently. Charles confessed that because he was the one selected as a replacement for none other than the infamous Bad-Ass Butch Cooper, that somehow made Charles feel like a badder, bad-ass guy than Butch."

Charles further explained, "By being the one to replace Butch as a center-fielder, that, in and of itself, promoted me to the position of top dog on the ball field, or anywhere on the playground, or anywhere in the entire school for that matter." Having heard all of this, his wife said, "Yes, but you aren't a bad-ass kind of guy. If I thought you were, I wouldn't have married you." She then said, "And, tell me something – if you were suddenly such a bad-ass, how is it that you were the one who was punched in the stomach?" Charles quickly raised the white flag; he knew when he was beat.

His ever-astute wife asked, "So, what is it really? You aren't a miserable guy and you're not a failure. You know what the problem is? You're bored. You need to find something, other than golf, to do with your time." Charles thought about what she had said and immediately outwitted her by actually stopping time for a moment (he has this ability) and racing forward, thus beating her to her anticipated punch line. "I'm not going to exercise in a public health club, if that's where you're going with this," he told her. "Fine", she said, "because I'm not going to cook anymore. And, I'm buying you a treadmill."

Charles decided that tomorrow he would re-start his neighborhood walking regimen. The blue skies had returned, and he was going to again find his way forward, into the future. And maybe a new ice cream flavor.

Mrs. Lewis

I have completed my moving endeavor and everything I own is now here, scattered throughout five rooms and a garage. My old place has been cleaned and the keys have, at last, been turned over to the realtor. In addition to my furniture, there are eighteen cartons that I will unpack one of these days when I'm better prepared to deal with the stressful inconvenience of starting life over, in a different house, in a different city. The cartons have been pushed to one side of the garage, while my Jeep occupies the other space.

I'm sitting here in the largest of the three upstairs bedrooms which I claimed as my permanent office. This room was obviously the designated master bedroom for the previous homeowner. However, my situation is such that I need acres of space in which to work, and only about six feet by four feet of mattress area in which to sleep; therefore, I chose one of the smaller bedrooms for sleeping. My desk and my laptop are placed in front of a window that faces the house directly across the street which is another two-story Craftsman, very similar to my place; the only difference being that my front porch is screened-in and the porch across the street is not. Mrs. Lewis lives there.

From what I have seen so far, it appears that Mrs. Lewis doesn't use her front door. I say this because I always see her entering and exiting from the side. I surmised that perhaps there is a large piece of furniture blocking the front door – a sofa or a TV maybe. And while her porch has some of the typical wicker furniture you would expect to find on a porch, I've never seen her sitting there, enjoying her morning coffee or relaxing in the evening breeze. Yesterday I saw a stray cat sleeping peacefully on the rocking-chair cushion, so maybe stray animals have been enjoying her porch. Not Mrs. Lewis, though.

Given that my workspace faces her house, I tend to observe a lot. Such as the fact that I have never seen any lights on anywhere in the house, regardless of the hour of the day. There's never been a mail delivery, or pickup, from her mailbox, nor a newspaper delivered, thrown irreverently at her driveway or sidewalk. While Mrs. Lewis appears to be old enough to be retired, every day I see her leave the house, through the side door, at ten minutes past seven, and I see her returning every afternoon at twenty minutes past four, which indicates that she might be catching the number 10 Market Heights bus. On the weekends, though, she is ever the hermit.

This evening, as I was sitting at my desk, I looked across the street to see the house totally dark, as usual, and it occurred to me that maybe Mrs. Lewis rents a single room on the backside of the house and that maybe I simply can't see her window light from my vantage-point on this side of the street. I decided it was time to take a break, so I stretched my legs, and made a fresh pot of coffee. While the coffee was brewing, I decided to pass the time and walk around the block to have a look at the back side of the house. I gave my very best impersonation of a neighbor out for a casual evening stroll, but found no rooms lit at the back of Mrs. Lewis' house where I had hoped to find one.

This morning I didn't see Mrs. Lewis leave her house at her usual time, and I didn't see her returning at her usual time in the afternoon either. Given that I had observed the same behavior from her since I had moved in, I was a bit unsettled. I kept an eye on Mrs. Lewis' driveway for nearly the entire day and saw no trace of her. I decided that first thing tomorrow, I would take a look and if nothing else, see if I saw a body on the floor. Around 8:00 the next morning, after again not seeing Mrs. Lewis leave according to her schedule, I walked across the street and stopped at the side door. I was surprised to see that there was no curtain on the side-door window. The window glass was filthy both outside and inside. Looking straight ahead, I was able to see all the way down the basement stairwell and part of the basement floor. The field of vision extended for about ten feet on either side of the stairwell. I didn't see a body on the floor, but did, however, notice a light switch on the wall just inside the side door. The switch was in the on position so the bulb must have burned out – that explained why I had never seen the side door light on.

Looking to my right, I saw two steps leading up to an open doorway that led into the kitchen. The kitchen was bare. I saw nothing there – no stove, no refrigerator, or anything else that we would expect to see in a typical kitchen. With more effort, I was able to see a very small portion of what I supposed could be a dining room. I walked around to the front of the house and onto the shabby, dusty porch. I saw that the front door window and the two living room windows were lacking curtains as well – more filthy windows, same as the side door. There was nothing in the living room. Absolutely nothing to be seen anywhere on the ground-floor of this house. The house was obviously vacant.

As I was turning to leave the porch and head home, I heard a voice call out, "Hey! What are you doing? Get the hell outta there or I'll call the cops!"

There was a man standing in his front yard at the house next to Mrs. Lewis' house – a smallish, bald guy wearing a wife-beater undershirt and tan Romeo slippers. "Go on! Get outta there!" he yelled. I walked across the driveway and approached him for the purpose of explaining my presence at the house, but he wasn't going to listen to what I had to say. As he turned and walked toward his door, I called to him, "Sir, I'm not here to cause problems. I'm concerned because I think Mrs. Lewis might be in some kind of trouble in there." He replied, "Who? There ain't nobody in there. There ain't no Mrs. Lewis around here. You better just go away or I'll call the police – you're trespassing!" I explained that, in fact, there was a Mrs. Lewis and I asked him how he could possibly not be aware of that simple fact. To this comment he said, "Well, I know there ain't nobody there because that's my rental property, but I don't rent it out anymore. Are you crazy or something? Who the hell is Mrs. Lewis?" Thoroughly confused and mildly annoyed, I shrugged and told him, "Yes, maybe you should just call the cops and we'll get this straightened out." He went into his house and slammed the door. I went across the street to my house.

I called the police, identified myself and explained the entire situation – Mrs. Lewis and her comings and goings, the absence of lights and furnishings in the house, etc., and I asked the dispatcher if he would send someone out to my house and perhaps they could check Mrs. Lewis' house, suggesting that she might be in there, ill or dead. Half an hour later, a Detective O'Malley rang my doorbell. We were sitting at my kitchen table, having coffee, and he was asking some questions about Mrs. Lewis – Who was she? How did I know her? Why would I think that she might be in some kind of trouble? I told him that, actually, I didn't know her. I explained that I'd never talked to her and that my only association with her was seeing her every day on the sidewalk as she walked to and from the bus stop. O'Malley paused and asked, "You never saw her anywhere else? Never talked to her? How do you know that she was on her way to work if you never talked to her?" I told him that I assumed she was going to work because she always left at the same time every morning and returned every afternoon at the same time. I explained that she always went to a bus stop, two blocks up the street. O'Malley probed further, "If you have never talked to this woman, how do you know that her name is Lewis?" I told him that I had seen the plaque beside her front door. The plaque said, "3125 Helen Lewis" and he said, "Are you sure? What kind of plaque is it?" Now that I was starting to feel uncomfortable, I raised my voice a bit and told him, "Hell, I don't know what kind of plaque it is. What does that even mean? It's a plaque -, the top line says 3125, the bottom line says Helen Lewis. Is that what you mean?" To my sarcasm, he the detective calmly replied, "Let's you and me take a walk over there and you can show me the plaque."

As we were walking across the street toward the house, I noticed that Romeo Slipper guy was sitting on his porch, watching O'Malley and me. We went up the porch steps and approached the front door. I was about to show O'Malley the plaque hanging on the wall to the left of the door, but then I noticed there was no plaque there. There should have been a plaque there. I've seen that plaque many times. How else would I have known this woman's name? I could only say, "Lewis, dammit, her name is Lewis; I'm not crazy. There was a plaque here." I pointed to the exact spot where the plaque had been. O'Malley said, "But there is NO plaque here. That's what I see. That's what I know. I don't see a plaque here." I moved in a little closer to the wall and I looked closely at the wall. "What the hell?" I noticed the two holes, eye-level, about 12 inches apart, exactly where that plaque had been. "Look! Right there! See the holes?" Detective O'Malley moved forward until he was perhaps two feet from the wall, never taking his eyes away from the place where a plaque had been. "Yep! I see them. I see the holes. Someone has removed that plaque. Good work!"

O'Malley squatted down and inspected the floor area directly under where the plaque had been attached to the wall. "Look at this!" He said, "Wood flakes and shingle debris on the floor. Someone has backed the screws out of this wall – almost certainly a recent act, otherwise these flakes would have been blown away by now." Using his phone, he snapped some pictures of the holes beside the door and the wood flakes on the porch floor. O'Malley said, "Did you notice that guy sitting on his porch when we crossed the street? And, did you notice that he went inside his house when he saw us looking at debris on the floor of the porch?" I told O'Malley that I saw him there on his porch, but I failed to notice that he had later gone inside his house. O'Malley asked me if I knew the guy and I told him that I did not. I explained that I had just moved into the neighborhood and didn't know any of the neighbors. I did tell O'Malley that the guy claimed to be the owner of the house, which he described as rental property. O'Malley said, "I think we need to have a chat with this guy."

We walked across the lawn to the neighbor's house; O'Malley pressed the doorbell. There was no response to the doorbell, so the Detective pushed the button again – twice. Still no response. O'Malley banged his fist on the door several times without a response from within. "Can I help you?" a new voice asked. Another neighbor had appeared in the front yard. My first thought was that he was probably just being nosey, and O'Malley would simply send him away, but my assumption was quickly proven wrong. O'Malley asked the guy if he knew the person that lived in this house, pointing to the door where we were standing. "Yes, I do know them. Arthur and Evelyn Lewis. Strange people, not very friendly." O'Malley glanced at me and then asked the man if it was a coincidence that the house next door to Arthur and Evelyn was also the home of a certain Helen Lewis. "Yes," he said, "Helen is Arthur's mother. She's been living in that house for years."

The detective and I returned to Helen Lewis' house and walked around the property for a while. When we came to the fenced-in backyard he lifted the gate latch and swung the gate open. When we came to the garage, I pointed out the frosted, side window and explained that the garage door window was frosted as well. We went back to the driveway and checked to see if the garage door was locked. Upon closer examination of the garage door and the side window, we discovered that the garage door had been caulked closed and painted over; also, the side window, and the side door on the other side of the building. I'm not sure why someone would do something like caulking a door and/or window to seal the openings, but I was sure that something is terribly wrong here.

"Let's go back to your place, shall we?" O'Malley said. We exited the backyard and he re-latched the fence. O'Malley didn't come in, explaining that he was going to make some calls and get authorization to do well-checks on both residences. He thanked me for my assistance. I thanked him for his allowing me to accompany him. I felt like a very important guy – a detective-in-training, perhaps. About three hours later, O'Malley returned, followed by a forensic van. They parked in the driveway and went to work.

I am now sitting in my favorite chair, on my screened front porch and I am watching Arthur and Evelyn Lewis, both in handcuffs, being stuffed into the back seat of a black and white police cruiser. They are on their way to jail where they will await a hearing. As it turns out, there was no Mrs. Helen Lewis living next door to her son and daughter-in-law. The real Mrs. Lewis – Arthur Lewis' mother – had been deceased for more than a decade. Her body was discovered inside a non-functional freezer chest which was located inside the detached garage in the backyard. Apparently, the freezer was the only thing that Arthur Lewis could find that would serve the purpose of a make-shift coffin.

The woman that I had seen walking up and down the sidewalk, five days a week, was Arthur Lewis' wife, Evelyn. Surprising fact: Mr. and Mrs. Lewis spent the better part of a year digging a tunnel through their basement wall, then under the driveway, and then through the basement wall of Arthur's rental property that was once the home of his mother but had been vacant for approximately twelve years. Every morning, Evelyn Lewis would dress as an older woman and then go through the tunnel, into the vacant rental house. Once inside the basement, she would go upstairs and exit by the side door, walk down the driveway to the sidewalk, and you already know the rest of her routine, except she didn't board the bus. Instead she walked to the next block and returned to her real home by cutting through a vacant lot from the next street over and then into her backyard. Then, in the afternoons, she would repeat the process, but reversed.

So, why go to all this trouble – the tunnel, the sidewalk, the bus stop, the secrets? The answer is even more bizarre than the story: The elder Mrs. Lewis had a tragic accident. As the story goes, she had been carrying a basket of laundry down the basement steps and, unfortunately, she lost her footing and tumbled downward to her eventual death. Arthur Lewis, mental giant that he is, decided that rather than calling the authorities as normal people would have done to properly dispose of the body, instead he and his wife would simply hide the body and continue receiving her monthly social security checks. As Helen's caregivers, they had full access to the funds which were regularly and electronically deposited into Helen's checking account. During the night, they wrapped her body in plastic and dragged it to the garage. They placed the body into the non-functional freezer chest and sealed the lid with duct tape. All for a few hundred dollars a month.

Sad? Very. True? Maybe.

Day After Day

This isn't working for me anymore. You can't just show up here, day after day, unannounced. The least you could do is give me an occasional heads-up to let me know that you're on your way. Is that too much to ask? I have to work; I have things to do – why can't you understand that? I have to beg your cooperation every day of my life. You can be unbearable sometimes – most of the time, actually.

Look, I understand your situation, I really do. But there's nothing I can do to help you. You must learn to help yourself. You must accept responsibility for your own life. I can't change your life, that's your job and you know I'm right – I know you do. Yet here you are, and you'll be here tomorrow, and the day after tomorrow, and every day, maybe forever if I don't stop you now. Your incessant jabbering is making me crazy. Jabber, jabber, jabber. You're getting on my nerves. I love you but I can't continue living like this. You're ill-mannered and you know I can't tolerate that. I should never have brought here in the first place.

I might as well just say it – I hate the way you look at me sometimes. You have this irritating way of cocking your head sideways and staring at me. And then, there are those unnerving, unblinking eyes of yours. You repeat the same actions – cock your head, don't blink and stare, over and over. It infuriates me. Actually, it frightens me, if you want to know the truth. You know what else bothers me? I can't bear the way you strut back and forth. You strut and then you cock your head to one side or the other and stare at me, like you're daring me or taunting me. Well, be careful, that's all I'm going to say – you've been warned!

You know, if you would at least be respectful of me we probably wouldn't be having this conversation right now. All I ask is that you just show some respect. I think you're capable of showing respect but you're stubborn and you won't. You just won't. I respect you. I don't strut back and forth, staring, unblinking at you. I take care of you and I worry about you, and you know why? It's because I respect you and I love you. Regardless of the difficulties you have put on me, I still have respect for you. What happened? What the hell happened?

~ ~ ~

Well, okay, if that's the way you feel, I will apologize. I apologize for everything. I'm sorry. Truly, I didn't know that you felt this way about me and about our relationship. How can you not be aware that I respect you – if I didn't respect you, or care about you, or love you, I wouldn't come here every day. I had no idea that I was "getting on your nerves." I was under the impression that you were okay with my visits. Look, I will stop coming here if that's the way you want it. And when did I ever ask you to step in and change my life? When? You said, "I can't change your life." Here's a suggestion for you – Don't! I don't want my life changed. I like my life just the way it is.

I didn't know that you have a problem with me staring at you with my "unblinking" eyes. Or, cocking my head. That makes you angry with me? I look at you? That's a bad thing now? That "frightens" you now? And now you are suggesting that I need to give you a heads-up when I'm on my way? When did you become the king of the castle? Apparently, I missed the announcement.

I appreciate the food, but I won't starve without your handouts. I eat the food because I'm under the impression that you felt the need to "take care of me." Really, don't waste your time. I'm perfectly capable of providing my own food. To be honest, I really don't want your handouts. I don't need handouts. And, oh my God, you think of *me* as "ill-mannered?" Me? You really need to get a grip on reality, my friend.

Look, it's time. It's time that you and I have "the conversation" about – everything. With the thought in mind that *you* think I started this entire thing, I must suggest to you that before you start on that subject, you need to get our relationship in perspective. I didn't come into *your* home and throw a towel over your body and take you away. You sent that dreadful idiot scurrying up the tree to snatch me from the nest. Yes, you saved my life and I will be forever in debt to you for that. Yes, my mother was killed by a car while finding food for me, and without my mother I would have starved. But you saved me. Have you ever thought that perhaps I come here every day to show my appreciation for your kindness, and here you are, sitting in there on your imaginary throne, hiding behind your precious window, proclaiming that I need to change my life?

I wasn't a problem for you all those months when I was hopping behind your heels as I followed you around the yard. And you always enjoyed watching me walk in circles around your lawn chair, amusing you – not stalking you. And what about the time you hid shiny objects in your rain gutter, and you found those shiny things a week later hidden behind the garage in the woodpile. And you praised me for being "so smart." And what about those treasurers I left for you behind the garage?

~ ~ ~

Big deal – any old crow could do that.

~ ~ ~

Twenty-two hours later:

Peck, peck. Tap, tap.
What!?
Open the window. Let me in.
NO!
I'm sorry.
No, you're not.
Open it!
NO!
O P E N it!!
NO!!

And there you have it . . . on and on it goes. This is what I must live with day after day. I'm thinking that I might have to remove the window ledge. I don't want to, but it might come to that if things don't change.

Allison Cried

(A Vignette)

Allison wasn't a happy girl when she was young, but later in her life, many years later, she came to understand that she was a kind and decent person; a person completely undeserving of cruel and disrespectful treatment. You see, Allison was a badly damaged young woman. Something awful happened in her life and, as a result of this misfortune, she lived most of her youthful years in a state of deep and desperate loneliness, a consequence of her self-imposed guilt. But despite her loneliness, Allison always tried to be as kind as she possibly could be. Despite it all, she never lost her ability to show kindness and consideration for others. Allison's kindness was ridiculed and, unfortunately, seen always as a weakness to be further exploited. Allison was stuck in a deep, dark hole and she had come to accept this unfortunate circumstance as her intended destiny. How unfortunate - pathetic even, you could say. Still, she was a courageous young woman and she never stopped in her efforts to improve her life situation. She never gave up.

Then one day, Allison was told something simple that was life changing. After one simple philosophy was shared with her, she finally came to understand that *she* was not the source of her problem, but, rather, the problem was the result of other peoples' blind hatefulness and shameful ignorance. Allison had asked this person-the-philosopher to teach her the art of smiling, and in doing so, this person showed her the light in the darkness of loneliness that had consumed Allison her entire life. The person assured Allison that there is no art or special skills involved in smiling, and that smiling is what people do when they have happiness in their heart.

The person also told Allison that if her heart is always joyful, her face will *always* be smiling. Allison thought for a few moments, recalling some of the things that she had seen in various life situations. She thought of puppies playfully tumbling in the grass, and she thought of running in the cool breezes of early April, and she thought of a beautiful sunset on the far ocean horizon and she thought of the autumn leaves – red, yellow, pink, purple, such amazing beauty. And then she cried, because crying was the only outward expression of emotion she had ever experienced. People have been known to cry, you know, when experiencing the awesome emotion of intense, overwhelming happiness.

Alison cried. Allison reclaimed her rightful place in this difficult world. And then she smiled.

www.ingramcontent.com/pod-product-compliance
Lightning Source LLC
Chambersburg PA
CBHW061239170626
46809CB00007B/2748

9781951940126